The Dan Marmor Mystery Box Presents:

Punching Ghost Nazis

Punching Ghost Nazis

Dan Marmor

Sad Sad Productions, LLC
2018

First Edition: 2018

ISBN: 978-1-73200-920-2

Sad Sad Productions, LLC
1214 Sanborn Ave
Los Angeles, CA 90029

www.danmarmor.com

Dedication

This book is dedicated
to those who punch their demons
right in the dang face!

Chapter 0

"I'll have you know, I have no idea what I'm doing," I said calmly, fully intending this sentiment to mean both in conversation and in the ways of normal life.

"That's fine, as long as you get the rent in on time and keep it quiet," said Bobby. He was a 22-year-old commercial real-estate investor. He had started in college renting out his dorm room on Airbnbee. Five years later he was renting out a dingy first-floor office in a corporate warehouse in the middle of Downtown Los Angeles to me. Me of all people. An office to me, for my business. My paranormal investigative operation.

"You know what? I'll call it The Dan Marmor Mystery Room," I said as I looked at the cracked walls and the wooden desk.

"*Really* don't care," Bobby replied curtly, already turning on his heel, making his way out of the door with the paperwork and my security deposit.

The young landlord left giving me time to ponder. And, just as I was about to let my brain rest from its long day of thinking, I saw it. It was under my nose all along.

I looked down, and in my arms, there was a corrugated cardboard box that held my most prized belongings. It was such a good box. This one box had made it possible for me carry my desk-toppers, accoutrements, gizmos, and gadgets into this new office space.

It hit me. I'd been holding exactly what the name of my new supernatural detective agency should be called...

THE DAN MARMOR *MYSTERY* BOX!

Chapter 1

"Did you have to choose that wonky font for *Mystery*, sir?" Simon said. You'll meet Simon in the paragraph following my response.

"How else will people know this venture is of the supernatural variety?" I responded coolly. "Anyhow, it's my sign and I'll do what I want with it." I sat on my new Seville chair, kicking my legs up onto the cracking desk before me. The chair was the most expensive piece of furniture in the room. Lumbar support. Fine leather. Gold buttons. $90 on Craigslist.

"Sounds really... well... I don't mean to offend, sir, but... dumb, sir," Simon said. This is Simon. Simon is a British computer genius from Cambridge. He always calls me sir because he's polite and British. He has a mustache that reminds me of Thomas Sellick. He created most of our ghost-hunting equipment. He's proved himself invaluable since we met by, well, sticking around.

"Oh, it is. Mind you, I have no idea what I'm doing," I reminded him.

"You've reminded me of that many times already, sir," Simon said. He does this thing when he's skeptical where he chews at the corner of his mustache, a big, hefty thing that hangs on his upper lip like a frozen, furry caterpillar.

I adjusted my jade tiger souvenir, which I had purchased during a trip to Thailand. It supposedly held the ghost of the Seua Saming, the spirit of a Thai woman in a black dress with legs as long as bamboo stalks who, during the full moon, searches for a man to accompany her for the night, proceeds to fornicate with her victim, turns into a tiger after the night's festivities, and devours him. Kind of like a sexy werewolf. Or a cannibalistic nymphomaniac.

Sounds weird, huh? But I wear the Seua Saming because I can relate.

Hear me out.

After a long hunt, I never let my paranormal victim escape. Rest assured I never try to bang spirits. Or there was this one time, but that's a story for another occasion and, in the meantime, I promise it wasn't anything too alarming.

I just jam the spirits I catch into inanimate objects. This is as I was taught to do by my mentor who just so happened to be my father, as he was taught by his mentor, and so on and so forth back to Medieval times, which is when this kind of thing first became my family's legitimate profession. That's where the name Marmor comes from. It was changed at Ellis Island when my family first migrated to America. In Czechoslovakian, it means *Dead Things Catcher*. Not anymore, but it did at one point. Now, it just means *marble* in Italian. But, I'm not one iota Italian, and I have never once played a game of marbles to completion.

"What are you thinking about, sir?" Simon asked. He could always tell when I was in reverie, engaged in some long form monologue in my head regarding a previous case or personal issues. "The Seua Saming, sir?" he asked.

"One thought behind, Simon. But perceptive nonetheless," I said feeling triumphant in my nostalgia. I swiveled in my chair and stood to look out of our new window, across the vast wet asphalt parking lot that extended before me.

The scent of the filth and grime of Los Angeles wafted through a small crack in the window. Smelled of urine.

"Smells like urine," I said aloud.

"Very perceptive, sir."

"I wonder why," I continued. "Maybe, it's the air pollution, or quite possibly we're positioned over a shallow sewer line.

"Look down, sir," Simon said sheepishly.

I looked down, and at my feet, leaning against the glass pane that separated the room from the outside world was a homeless man, behind a planter, urinating. He looked at me and smiled a toothless grin and didn't stop peeing until he was done. Not one bit ashamed to be caught in the act.

"You know… you might be correct. That's most likely the cause of the pungent aroma."

"I think, sir. I… " Simon began to say, but he trailed off, which he is known to do when excited, flabbergasted, or flustered.

While looking over the growing pool of piss at my feet, the decrepit landscape, and the boring flatness of this anonymous LA parking lot, drenched in sun and excretions, I waited for him to pick up right where he left off, but he didn't. Instead, I heard soft but poignant taps against the wooden floor, growing louder as they approached. I quickly deduced that these taps might be the sounds of footsteps approaching, or a haunted slinky.

I turned, as I'm wonted to do when I hear footsteps approach me from behind. A common reaction. One that most people might have when they hear a sound approaching them from the rear. Is it a Pavlovian response? Or is it biological? Maybe, it's just habit. A curse of my deadly curiosity.

The click-clack along the wood went click clack as the footsteps approached. So, I turned. I turned as any man would do in this situation as I discussed just before, if you'll recall, the reactionary measures most people take when responding to an encroaching entity making progress from the back.

"Good morning, Mr. Marmor," a voice said as I was still in the process of completing my one-hundred-and-eighty-degree revolution. It was a feminine voice. I could tell from it being higher-pitched than most male voices. It could have been a young boy's voice, but it had gravitas, poise. Thus, I assumed based on the data that I was receiving through my ears that this was a female's voice. The voice breathy and low, like one might hear in a movie where the character is played by a woman. Thus, I drew the conclusion that it had to, therefore, be a woman.

And lo, when I completed my turn and faced the visitor, I was certainly correct. It was a woman. Astute as ever, I knew that my skills as a detective were still at their peak.

She wore a black dress, open at the thigh, cut high on her right leg. Her hair was jet black as well. Her purse, black. Her shoes, black. Her lipstick, black. Her mascara, black. Her skin, black. She was like a walking silhouette with bright, white teeth and a smile that gave me goosebumps. I could tell she was going to speak. The way her lips started to part. The way she inhaled. The way she let words come out of her mouth, literally the definition of speaking.

"I need your help," she said

There it was. I was right again. She had spoken.

Chapter 2

"I would offer you a seat," I said, "but as you can see, we're just moving in," I said as I sat in my Seville chair. Then realizing that she would remain standing if I continued sitting, I stood again. I rolled the swivel chair around the desk so that I could place it behind her. Simon's eyes were wide. He was in awe of her beauty.

"I'm sorry," I said. "As you can I see, I have no idea what I'm doing."

As she sat, she leaned towards my ear and whispered, "That's not what I heard."

I knew then she was trouble.

"Did you just call me trouble?" she asked, crossing her legs and staring up at me, through her wide eyes that seemed to be solid black. I looked at Simon and pleaded with my eyes: did I just say that out loud? Simon nodded in the affirmative, mouth still agape.

"Trouble has many definitions," I said in lieu of apologizing as I walked back to my side of the desk. I don't ever apologize. Sorry isn't in my vocabulary, except of course when I have to explain that the word isn't a part of my vocabulary. To clarify, of course I know the word sorry. I understand its meaning. I just refuse to use it in everyday vocabulary. I don't apologize often is what I'm trying to say. "As you might already know from my reputation, I don't deal with cheating spouses, missing children, or murders most foul. I only deal in…"

"The supernatural," she said finishing my sentence, "I know, Mr. Marmor. I've done my research." She pulled a black pearl cigarette case from her black purse, opened it with a black fingernail, and put a thin, black cigarette to her lips, waiting for a light.

"I'll get you a light," I said realizing that she expected me to get her a light. I had brought one just for this very occasion and placed it in the top drawer of my new desk. I pulled at the drawer, but it didn't budge. "Just a moment," I said. I pulled harder.

"Damn thing!" I pulled as hard as I could, opening the jammed drawer and falling flat on my rear end, spilling the contents of the drawer onto the carpet around me. I pulled myself up, white-knuckling the edge of the desk until I could peek over the tabletop with my lighter in hand. I lit her cigarette with my Zipo lighter, an artifact I inherited from my father. Inscribed on the side: *Between the afterlife and the beforelife lies life itself.* My father was a damned good ghost-hunter. In his day, the family business was booming. Today, people read *Scientific Americana* and believe that ghosts are mere fables told by religious fanatics. Little do they know what lurks in the shadows, what hides in the transparent spaces between now and later, what waits in the dimensional planes that link us to our celestial traces.

She puffed, inhaled, and let the smoke pour from her lips, upwards towards the ceiling, where the broken fan hung limply.

"If you don't mind, sir…" Simon said, taking initiative and turned to the woman, "how'd you hear about us?" Simon asked. "We just picked up again."

"I was referred. My friend, Stephen Mills, a pilot. He and I were, how do I say it, close." She brushed her hair from her eye as she spoke, revealing that she had complete heterochromia, one eye black and one eye light blue, almost as pale as her pupil. "He recently passed, but on his death-bed, he told me I should find you, Mr. Marmor."

"I remember him well," I said. He'd been my first client when I was starting out. A friend of my father's. My father, mind you, disappeared years back. As soon as I caught my first ghost if, he vanished. He had said he was going out for Milk, not the drink but rather a ghost in the diary section at Ralphy's Grocery Store. And, he never came back. That was twelve years ago. Stephen Mills was at his funeral. He told me that my father had handled a haunted propeller for him. Easy to lose a finger or even a hand with a haunted propeller, but he managed to stabilize the engine, un-phantom the propeller, and even give the single person flyer a quick oil change. He was a full-service detective, after all. I still had the voucher for one free flight out of it, which I had never used.

"Sir," Simon said.

"Hmm?" I responded. I had been in one of my reveries again. Reminiscing about Stephen Mills, the pilot. "When did he pass?"

"Last night," the woman said and smoked. "I think something was out to get him, and it may be turning its attention on me."

"And who are you?"

"My name is Blanche," she said. "Blanche Black. I need you to come over and investigate at once."

"I'm not that easy."

"I can pay." She pulled out her wallet, but it was empty. "Don't worry. There's money in it for you," she continued.

"I'm expensive," I said trying to mimic her breathy tone, "and I could use the cash. Rent's due on the first of every month. But, still not sold. Could be a mad neighbor, a jilted lover, an ex-customer, a rival pilot, a piteous plot propagated by some pitiful preacher posing a problem, pretending to be a poltergeist, or it could just be a possum, Blanche."

"There's something in my house, Mr. Marmor. Something strange. Something mysterious. Something supernatural," she said.

"You've piqued my interest," I went to sit on my Seville chair only to realize that it wasn't there when I fell back onto my rear end again. It would definitely be bruising. I pulled myself up and brushed myself off, "But, what is it?"

"It's some kind of transparent vision. I can't always see it, but I can hear it. Stephen said it was out to get him before he, well, croaked," Blanche said with barely a blink.

"An apparition," I clarified.

"I haven't been able to sleep. I can't work. I can barely do my face. It's just..."

"Annoying," I said.

"Exactly," she responded.

"Quite perceptive, sir," Simon said.

"I need it gone," she continued.

I considered the proposal. We needed the money, and this was a promising case. She eyed me as smoke drifted up her sharp cheekbones. I could see she was thinking about the question she had just delivered. Waiting for an answer. So, I gave her one.

"An annoying apparition." I pointed at Simon, proud of my alliteration, who looked at me like he'd been thrust onto a stage in his underwear.

She snuffed her cigarette out on my desk, the ashes pooling around the tip of the cigarette as she stood. It was a new desk, but I didn't say anything about it. I knew then I'd have to invest in an ash tray. Maybe I could steal one from her apartment. Which meant we'd have to take the case, after all.

"Excuse me?" she said.

"Sir," Simon said. I eyed him again and begged again: did I just say that aloud? He nodded. I had.

"Nothing," I said.

She eyed me beneath her furrowed brow and reluctantly pulled out her business card. "I'll be expecting your call," she said and she turned for the door. The familiar click-clack of her black high heels went click clack as she walked out of the door.

I called after her, "I'll remind you. I have no idea what I'm doing."

She stopped and stared at me with her one dark eye. "I know," she said, "but you're the best chance I've got, Mr. Marmor." She continued leaving, but I stopped her before she could make it fully out of the door.

"Call me Dan," I said. She stopped one last time at the doorway. Looked at me. I could tell she was going to speak by the way she inhaled, by the way her dark lips parted.

"No," she said and left.

I went to sit, to contemplate her proposal and again fell flat on my backside. I knew then that I'd need to invest in more chairs. This business was about get expensive.

"How about we get a drink," I said pulling myself up again.

"It's ten in the morning," Simon said.

"Right. I apologize. A few drinks."

Chapter 3

La Dorada bar is an old Western kind of bar on South Spring Street, Los Angeles. I wouldn't call it a dive bar unless I'm in there because I probably would never speak about it aloud without being there. I have never once been in a position where I had to describe it to anybody. It doesn't usually open until 5 pm, but Marc, a bartender there, is a friend of mine and also likes to imbibe as much as I do. He's a photographer from Somerville who knows his way around a wraith sighting or two. Marc's a red-headed man with a full, red beard. I have always been jealous of the fullness of his beard. It rivals the fullness of Simon's mustache. Meanwhile, my inability to grow facial hair of any kind, except for wisps of chin hair and a few blondish strands on my upper lip, made me feel inadequate in all settings surrounded by these two hairy-faced chaps.

"So, what did she smell like?" Marc asked as he passed us our drinks. Long Island Iced Teas with the little umbrella. That's my drink. Always has been. Always will be.

"Cigarettes," I said as I licked the bottom of the mini umbrella's mini pole. The drink was sweet and tangy and delicious. Marc's Long Island Iced Teas are award-winning. Or have won one award. I myself gave them the BDOTY Award. The Best Drink of The Year Award. I've given it to other drinks this year but Marc doesn't need to know that.

"Perceptive, sir," Simon said.

"What?" I said. Then I remembered what we were talking about. "So she's got an apparition in her apartment. Now, how are we supposed to find it if we don't even know where she lives. I didn't even ask for her address!" I said, drinking.

"She gave you her card, sir," Simon reminded.

"Truer words have never been spoken, but it would have been a nice ice-breaker anyhow," I said. "Chivalrous questioning is still important even in these modern times. They say chivalry is dead, but I say ghosts are dead." I reflected for a moment. "I don't know about chivalry."

"You don't know anything," Marc said casually, toasting with a gesture, not with a clink.

"You're right," I said. "I have absolutely no clue. And have never claimed to. In fact, I claim the opposite."

"With an almost annoying frequency," said Marc.

"You're the befuddled banshee beater, sir," Simon said.

"The dumb demon destroyer," Marc said.

"The pinheaded poltergeist punisher, sir," Simon said.

"The vexing visitor villain," Marc said.

"The sad spook slayer, sir," Simon said

"Okay. I get it," I said. "Another please." I handed my empty glass back to Marc and watched as he mixed the cocktail with his notorious flair.

"So, you gonna take the job?" Marc asked giving me my second.

"I don't want to."

"You don't want to do anything, sir," Simon said. "Ever."

"Yeah, man," Marc said, "but you need the money. Last time you were here you ate a whole lime, peel and all, for two bucks."

"You are right, my friend," I said taking the umbrella from my refill. Opening and closing it a few times, watching as the paper constrict and unfold delicately. "Maybe I should do it."

"Why wouldn't you?" Marc responded.

"I've been working out of my apartment for twelve years, been struggling to make ends meet. Finally, get access to my father's bank accounts, filed his supposed death certificate, and... you know, I don't even know if he's dead. For all I know, he could be the ghost haunting Blanche. Wouldn't that be an epic twist."

"Or, he could be dead. I mean you did have a funeral for him," Marc said.

"Without his body. I guess, you're right. I don't want to waste this chance. I don't want to do my father's memory wrong. I don't want to fail."

"Fear, sir, wreaks havoc on hope," Simon said. He sipped his drink and put it back, barely a taste, "and the last thing you should be, sir, if you don't mind me saying, is scared."

"Good point, I think," I said finishing the next drink.

"Are you taking it?" Marc asked.

I thought a moment, stirring the ice of my empty glass with the umbrella. It had been so long since I'd been on a case. After the last one, the one a year ago, the one that ruined me, the one that left me broken, shaking, home for three months in bed, watching television, and eating nothing but frozen treats and un-microwaved chicken nuggets. The microwave was broken, honestly, but if it hadn't been for Simon, or that telegram, I don't think I would have even been sitting where I was right then. But, these are all stories for another time.

"What telegram, sir?" Simon asked.

"Hmm?" I asked.

"You were talking aloud again, sir." Simon said.

"I must have been," I said. "I don't ever talk about the telegram."

Marc and Simon stared at me as I stirred the ice of my empty drink.

"Should I get my damn camera or what?" Marc asked.

"First, you get me one more of those good Long Island Iced Teas. Then you get your camera," I said and paused for a moment to build anticipation. "We're going to catch us a ghost!"

Chapter 4

If you've never listened to music by American Head Charge, I'd recommend that you take a moment and listen. Yes, you, reader. I am talking to you. Am I not allowed to break this wall and engage with you directly?

If you'd prefer to remain out of my ramblings, please contact me or my estate (depending on when you are reading this) directly, and I, or my estate, will offer you an insincere apology.

Please, now, put on American Head Charge. Find it online. It's simple. Specifically, the album "The War of Art." Specifically, the song "Pushing the Envelope." Take a moment, and listen to this song, or an hour to listen to the full album. But, not just listen. Blast it. Use your Bluetooth speakers. Crank this music to full volume. For you to entirely immerse yourself within this chapter, it's imperative that you understand the genre of music known as industrial metal and how listening to industrial metal at extreme volumes can be both cathartic and obnoxious.

My colleagues and I, as we do before every good mystery, blasted this album in our new office. I packed my mystery box with all of my accoutrements. My spyglass. My pocket-watch. My crystals. My gas-spectrometer. My protein bar. My hand mirror. My bait and switch mechanism. My porcelain orb, my toothbrush just in case there was an overnight stake out, and of course... my Ghost Mittens™. My big, red, electrically engineered, ghost-punching gloves that can knock the socks off of any being.

Drink in hand, Marc somehow managed to remain standing while head-banging to the music. He's heard this album hundreds of times, and he knows the words by heart. Already packed, Simon had earplugs in, and with legs delicately crossed, sat reading *Paradise Lost*. Took a moment to ponder a line of the poem. Eyed Marc as if he corroborated whatever thought briefly swam through his head, sighed. Then, gently turned the page and continued reading.

During the best part of the song, the ending, the bit with the extensive profanity, which I refuse to write here but adore to listen to, Bobby the 22-year-old landlord stormed in. He shouted something incomprehensible. I cupped my hand over my ear, gesturing to the young entrepreneur to indicate that I could not possibly hear him over the tinnitus-inducing level of the music. I continued packing my mystery box. My 10L-canister of liquid nitrogen. My night mask. My handheld camcorder, for posterity's sake. My Electromagnetic Field Meter. My mechanically powered flashlight.

Bobby screamed again. Alas, it was too loud. I couldn't hear a word he said.

Again, I cupped my hand to my ear as if to say, *What? I can't hear you!* Bobby stomped by the reading Simon and the dancing Marc as he stomped his way towards the location of the stereo.

As he stood in front of my speaker system, he turned back at me and glared. And then he pressed the power button with firm thumb ending the song at the best part.

Simon, unmoved, continued reading. Marc, dumbstruck by the sudden pause, stood slowly and puffed up his chest as if he were preparing for a fight. I took the lead on the situation, not wanting the conflict to escalate.

"You can't just blast music like that. It's loud," Bobby complained, trying to dig residual noise from his ear cavities with his index finger. As if noise could get stuck in ear wax. All for show. All theatrics. Bobby, the little drama queen.

"Excuse me? What did you call me?" Bobby said.

I looked at Simon, but he didn't see me. He was too engrossed in his book to answer whether I had spoken aloud. So, I incorrectly assumed I hadn't.

I held tall and looked at Bobby. And, for a moment, I felt bad. Almost guilty. Like I could and maybe should apologize. But apologies, sincere apologies, are not my strong suit. To pry an apology from me is like ripping an ice pick from a dead man's frozen hand on Mount Kilimanjaro. It's hard to do, and sometimes one must rip off the whole arm to get it. I find apologies weaken resolve. For instance, why apologize for having a nice conversation with a cashier. Just because there may be a line forming does not mean that a man needs to rush polite conversation with a barista or a clerk. No, I will not apologize for my human decency. No, I will not entertain sideways glances and keep my conversation to curt missives directed at employees of establishments I frequent. I will, and I repeat, I will indulge my tête-à-tête fancies however I please.

"What the hell are you talking about?" Bobby asked.

"Sir," Simon said without looking up from his book. "You're rambling again."

"Yes. Right." I walked towards Bobby who stared back at me, terribly confused. I could see it in his wide eyes, his furrowed brow, his pursed lips. I could see that he wanted to speak, that he wanted to continue to berate me. I stood before the young landlord, thinking, contemplating his existence, feeling superior. I doubt he had ever shaved. I, on the other hand, have to shave at least twice a month.

"We were just leaving," I said, and headed for the door.

"Sir," Simon said one more time pointing to the box.

"Need I remind you," I said not intending to finish the sentence.

"You don't know anything. I know, sir," Simon said sullenly, standing, and straightening his trousers. Together, Marc, Simon, and I walked to the door leaving the youthful, corporate slumlord to stew in his anger, as we shut the door behind us.

After all, we had an apparition to catch.

16

Chapter 5

Blanche lived on Myra Street in Silver Lake, a small, hip neighborhood east of Hollywood. She had a swanky apartment overlooking the city from the hill. We stood looking up at the glory that was Blanche's home. In the daylight, it didn't look so intimidating. In the daylight, ghosts are barely scary. They seem like a distant threat, sequestered to nighttime and shadows.

We made our way to the front gate, which held us at street level before a buzzer that read CALL. I pressed the button, Simon at my five and Marc at my seven. These numbers represent the locations of my companions relative to where I was standing. This system is commonly used by military personnel, police officers, and pilots. I use numbers sometimes to express how serious I am at my job.

We'd made a pit-stop at Marc's for his camera, a serious rig. You might mistake him for one a Hollywood type, that is, if you didn't know he was intent on photographing the un-seeable entities that float on the periphery of reality.

"Come up," a voice spoke through the intercom. I could tell it was Blanche because the voice through the intercom matched Blanche's voice from yesterday. Even without an introduction, I can place people's voices. I gave myself an A+ at that moment for detective work.

She knew we were coming. I could hear the vodka martini on her breath, turning her words into string of consonants, imperfectly enunciated, and it made me quite parched. We pushed through the gate and wandered up the concrete stairway. It smelled of lavender. I hate lavender.

Blanche's place was a lavish, lime-green building with a staircase that seemed to last forever. There were windows, huge bay windows, with a view of the Hollywood Sign and Griffith Observatory. I was already out of breath, and thus, despite Simon advising me to look back and soak in the view, I cautioned him that if he asked me one more time to look over my shoulder, I would collapse and topple backwards and subsequently take all three of us out. He retracted his counsel and opined that I should continue walking without attempting to look back. I did just that, but not because he told me to, but rather merely because that's what I would have done anyway.

However, Marc added, "Breathe in through the nose and out through the mouth, bro," to which I responded with a string of expletives I refuse to document here.

At the top of the stairs, I put my mystery box on the ground and held for a few moments with my hands on my knees to catch my breath. Fortunately for me, Marc had the forethought to bring his thermos. He handed it to me so I could swig from it, and I was pleasantly surprised to find that it was Long Island Iced Tea. Nothing quenches an insatiable thirst better than Marc's Long Island Iced Teas. For good measure, I handed the thermos to Simon but without cautioning him about its contents. Caught off-guard, Simon sent the drink spewing over the cacti and rock garden below.

Though I wanted to, I couldn't laugh. I was still searching for my breath, but I managed to slap him on the back, harkening to the joviality of jest amongst friends. But, Simon was not bemused. "Sir, I beg you. Next time, please tell me what it is you are drinking."

"From now on," I retorted, "always assume the worst. Need I remind you, I have no idea what I'm doing."

"You don't," Marc added.

"I'm well aware, sir. I'm sorry. I should not have assumed," Simon said.

"You know what they say about assuming, right?" I asked.

"No," Simon said. "What do they say?"

"I don't know. I was asking you," I said. "Let's get inside."

Marc was busy taking pictures of the foliage. His attention span something on par with that of a chicken. This might explain his inability to sustain a relationship. I would liken his dating habits to that of a fine-dining experience. He indulges greatly, but only so big a portion that he can sustain his ravenous eating for the next delicacy. If you've ever eaten at French's Laundry, or Per Say, do so in order to understand Marc's dating habits. I, unfortunately, have dined at neither, but that makes me no less aware of the rations and fine quality of the dining experience at the aforementioned restaurants.

"Sir," Simon said.

I straightened up. "Where were we?" I asked.

"You were about to say your tag-line, sir." Simon reminded.

"Yes. Of course." I cleared my throat. Puffed out my chest. Inhaled through my nostrils, and said, "Let's go." I'm not proud of it, but that's the best I could come up with when I was a child, and it stuck. My ghost-hunting motto. Maybe, one day I'll be able to have a better punchline, but for now it gets the job done.

And, we walked towards the door. I held out my hand, curled it into a fist, and gave one hearty knock. The wood was strong and firm and hurt my knuckles. I should have used the door knocker. It was a bronze-pineapple with a heavy piece of tarnished bronze hanging in such a way that made it look oddly testicular. Two round, smooth balls hung loosely from the oddly thin pineapple. "Quite phallic," I said aloud.

"Well deduced, sir." Simon said.

"Looks like a p-," Marc began to say until I cut him off.

"Please. No profanity," I said, "But, you're not wrong." I held the pineapple door knocker's bronze genitalia in my hand and was about to rap against the door with them when the door suddenly flew open. Marc snapped a picture, but he exclaimed as soon as it had been taken that it was underexposed.

"Hello?" I called. "Hello!" I said one more time. Nothing. No response.

"Shall we?" I asked my colleagues. They both shrugged. I knew then that it was up to me. I was the decisive vote. I was the champion of progress. I said, "Let's go," and we entered the house one by one.

Upon crossing the threshold, I could sense something odd. I found myself unconsciously gripping onto the edges of my mystery box, the cardboard slightly bending beneath my tightening grasp. We walked into the entryway atop a polished wooden floor beneath a glass Murano chandelier, pink roses cracking at the tips, all unlit. Cobwebs hung like lacy decorations between each stem. Our eyes scanned the room looking for any sign of people or anything out of the ordinary.

"Spooky," Marc said, getting uncomfortably close to Simon but still able to drink from his thermos. Simon tried to push him away to no avail. I know this not because I looked back but because this happens every time we go on a mystery. Marc likes to drink uncomfortably close to Simon just to make him feel awkward. Not sure exactly what pleasure he gets out of it. To each his own.

I held up a fist, ready for something to come at us, sensing something off. This gesture is a military gesture that means, HALT! I have learned to use it in my mystery hunts. It helps me feel more in control of my companions. Though they obviously have free will and can do as they please, in my experience, I have found that they understand the signal and often abide by it as if I were their sergeant. (I have no experience in the military, and I am glad that I can boast that I have only been shot at once. Another story for another time.)

"Sir. Why are we stopped?" Simon questioned.

"Oh right," I said and put my fist down so we could continue on.

We did just that. We continued on into the room, the floor creaking beneath our every step. Sounds seemed to reverberate from every corner of the house, as if the walls were cautioning us to turn around and leave. But I don't listen to inanimate object anymore. That was merely a phase in college that stemmed from experiments with chemical compounds. Another story for another time. At that point in my life, I had neither done enough research on nor been capable of embracing the effects of such compounds, what with my undiagnosed psychological disorders, at least one of which must be written about in every alphabetical section of the DSM V.

Just then, I heard footsteps. They were coming closer. I knew because the sound was getting louder. But, it wasn't the same click clack of the high heels that Blanche had worn in my office. The sound was rounder, fuller.

"Shoes," I said.

"Perceptive, sir,' Simon said.

We three, Marc, Simon, and me, we all huddled together. We were terrified of the ghost we might encounter. I gulped, worried about the forthcoming battle that I was severely unprepared for, out of practice, out of shape, and without a clue as to what I was doing. That's when we saw him. An old man. Grey mutton chops. Grey hair. A pipe in his mouth. Like a sailor but with a fancy sweater draped over his back and aviator glasses. "Who's here?" the old man bellowed.

"Simon," I said in a whisper, frozen with fear. "Do you see him?"

"Yes, sir," Simon said.

"Can you do an EMF reading?"

"On the man, sir?"

"On the ghost man. Yes."

"Are you certain?" he asked.

"Only fools are certain," I reminded him.

"You positive, sir?" Simon asked.

"I'm certain," I said.

Simon reached into his sack and pulled out the EMF reader. He slowly pulled it towards himself as to not upset the being before us. He turned it on, and it made a nice sound with an arpeggio of notes in D flat major, most likely. I don't know music theory — I had Simon program it for me so it no longer sounded as somber as its B flat original setting. And also my name starts with D, so I thought a D chord would be nice.

Simon walked towards the old man, holding the EMF reader with extended arm, trying to gauge his ghostly emissions. It beeped loudly and turned red for a moment. But this was just how it booted up. After the initial detection, it remained silent and held on green. The green light stayed lit as he approached. Simon got closer and closer, trying to keep his face as far back from his hand as he possibly could. Terrified as to what might happen to him, but Simon is a loyal sidekick (do not call him that to his face, or he will be sour for at least twenty minutes, and when Simon is sour, he barely speaks), and he continued onward toward the ghost. It was odd because said ghost was more opaque, more solid, than any other ghost I'd ever seen before.

Simon was within a foot of the being, and no reading. "Sir, I am not getting a reading," he whispered now less than a foot from the thing's face.

"Closer!" I suggested rather strongly as denoted by the exclamation point. Still in a whisper, but more of something like a stage whisper. It strained my vocal chords, and I was not happy that I had to undertake such an absurd display to get Simon to do my bidding. He would hear about this later in his post-mystery employee review.

Simon moved closer with the EMF reader, closer still, inching towards the thing's face until he lodged the EMF reader in the thing's mouth, alongside its pipe.

The thing raised its hand and smacked the device from Simon's fist to the floor. The EMF reader powered down instantly as its batteries flew from its compartment and across the floor into the adjacent room. Simon gave chase.

"I've had enough of your shenanigans. What in God's name are you doing here?" the ghost said.

It was a man. A real man, and I knew the man. I'd spoken with him before. He was a man whose name sat on the tip of my tongue, but it couldn't be. I'd had word that morning that he had died the day prior.

"Mr. Mills?!" I gasped.

"Astute, Danny. How in the hell are ya, boy?" Stephen said and extended his arms as he approached in order to give me a hug. I could feel that he was warm. His pulse was beating. His breath smelled of a sneeze. You know the smell. It lingers in the nostrils and smells like stale garbage. I parted from him as quickly as I could, but hugs are not easy to end abruptly.

I remembered at that moment, almost as if I was transported back to it, one hug that lasted for way too long. I had to give approximately nine pats on the back of the offending hugger to free myself from his grasp, and he took insult to my need for personal space. I remember thinking that this offensive hugger should be wrapped in a blanket so he could never have use of his arms again.

"The heck did you just say?"

I knew then even if I couldn't verify from Simon's horrified face that I'd spoken out loud. So, I adeptly changed the subject with the conversational grace of a figure skater.

"You're alive," I shouted as I thought I could use this realization to part, but he didn't let that break his grasp of me.

"Again. Astute, Danny. Quite the chip off the old block, let me tell ya," he said continuing the hug.

"Blanche said you were dead," I said, this time taking his arms from around my shoulders with my two hands and placed them back at his sides.

"If she meant hungover, then yes. She can be dramatic at times," he responded finally letting me be.

"Are you and Blanche like, a *thing*?" Marc asked, making a lewd gesture, holding the index finger on his right hand straight and culling his left hand's index finger to his left thumb to form a circle. He then pushed the straight finger directly into the circle he created, pulled it out, and in, and out, and in. Only after a few seconds did I realize what he was doing, and I slapped his hands to stop him from doing such a disgusting gesture.

Mr. Mills laughed. "Yessiree. I'm a lucky man."

"Damn right you are," Marc responded and held out his fist for a bump. Mr. Mills did not take him up on it.

"Come. Let's sit down. Shall we?" Mr. Mills guided us into the living room where we found Simon chin-deep under a sofa, reaching as best he could.

"What are you doing down there, digging for gold?" I asked, in an attempt to belittle him in front of Mr. Mills. Maybe, I was searching the approval I had never received from my father. But Mr. Mills didn't laugh. I didn't even think my joke was particularly clever, myself.

"Just reaching for a fallen battery, sir," Simon responded.

"It was a joke," I responded. "I was mocking you." I laughed again, looking to Mr. Mills for validation. I got none.

"Good one, sir," Simon said. "Good one."

"Help these days, am I right?" I said to Mr. Mills putting on airs, but he again didn't respond the way I'd hoped. He didn't even acknowledge my charm, wit, and hilarious timing.

"Can I get you anything to drink?" Mr. Mills said.

"Long Island Iced Tea, please. With a little umbrella," I responded.

"And me," Marc said, too.

"And some knee pads for my associate here," I said regarding Simon again in a joking manner. I laughed harder than I had before trying to get Mr. Mills' attention, but he didn't look.

"Excellent burn, sir. I will most undoubtedly need some lotion for it," Simon said.

With that, Mr. Mills burst into a fit of laughter. "Hoooweee, your friend is funny," he said. "I'll do my best on the drinks. I warn you I don't know how to make a Long Island Iced Tea." I stewed in silence until I realized that Mr. Mills must not know anything about comedy, either. I didn't want his approval.

"That's fine," I said.

Mr. Mills nodded and left the room.

Meanwhile, Marc and I sat on either side of Simon whose hand was still beneath the couch. We shared nips from the thermos as we waited for our fresh cocktails. The living room was a spectacle, bathed in light from the outside. Three modern couches, all different pastel colors. The chandelier was what you might find at a lounge, hanging by one wire, bare lightbulbs dimly lit as to not tamper with the beautiful natural light from outside. Family photographs sat on every available surface. A fire place on the rear wall, and over the mantel piece, a gigantic photograph, glossy, and well-mounted of Blanche, fully nude, reclining on a sofa, staring dead into the camera.

"I thought she said the old man was dead," Marc said.

"As did I," I said.

"What do you think that's about?"

"Not a clue. I dare not venture a guess before I get the facts, my dear dumb friend," I said.

"Bro, why are you talking like that?" Marc asked.

"Like what?" I asked.

"Like, I don't know, like a bitch," Marc said.

"How dare you call me such a term, especially in this house, especially so close to female company," I said, pointing at the picture. "I have not a clue what you mean, and I'll have you know, I do not appreciate that language. Not one bit," I was going to continue about the psychological effects of a dirty mouth when Simon's boot hit my foot with purpose.

"Sir, I hate to disturb you, but… " Simon started and subsequently finished, "I'm stuck."

"I want solutions here, not problems, Simon," I responded. That is my go-to line, especially when it comes to Simon.

"Could you, sir, not to be a burden, possibly pull me out?" Simon asked, his voice muffled by the sofa cushions beneath me.

Simon was then under the sofa and could very well be reaching for a cube of cheese. Just like a mouse. I began to grow fond of a Simon with big, floppy ears and a wiry pink tail. The image took my fancy. He would squeal instead of speaking. He would have two big buck teeth hanging over his bottom lip, and he'd live in my wall, in a small hole in the molding behind my desk. I could buy a wheel for him to run on and feed him water from a little bottle. He'd love his sunflower seeds and chew on them with his little buck teeth around the edges, gripping the seeds in his little paws. *D'aww.*

"Sir?" Simon said again.

"Yes! Right on it, Si-mouse... I mean, Simon. Of course. The human Simon." I stood. "Marc. If you please." I gestured for Marc to stand as well and pointed at Simon's right leg. I took up his left in my two arms.

"Sir, I don't think this is all necessary."

"Nonsense," I said. "On three. Pull." I planted my feet, bent my knees, and gripped his leg in my arms. His body was now horizontal over the floor, his arm still caught beneath. "One. Two."

But, before I could say three, Marc was already yanking at Simon's leg. So, I too began. "Who needs three?" I muttered under my breath as we wrenched at Simon's legs. We pulled and pulled, yanked, wretched, twisted, and jerked, until finally poor Simon's arm freed itself from beneath the couch, and we three went flying backwards. I fell onto my rear and knew that it would be black and blue by the morning.

I slid a good two feet on those polished floors, my bottom absorbing all of the impact, leaving me relatively unscathed except for my ego. And my butt.

When I looked up, I found myself staring upwards at the now black-skirted Blanche, who, from my vantage point, was wearing black, lace underwear.

"Long Island Iced Teas anyone?" she said staring down at me as Simon triumphantly replaced the battery in his EMF reader.

Chapter 6

We all sat on the loveseat together, me, Simon, and Marc. Simon in the middle. It would have been more alliterative to have Marc in the middle, but I only deal with truths. This is how it happened, and Simon was slammed in the middle. There we go. Compromise. We get alliteration and truth in one! Simon was smushed right in the center. Even better. His legs pressed together, his elbows jammed into the sides of his stomach, his hands awkwardly clasped on his lap. Meanwhile, I lounged with my legs spread, my Long Island Iced Tea, already on its third refill, leisurely set on the table to the side. Marc looked at his eyePhone, playing Dos Dots and not very well.

We faced Stephen Mills, the old aviation expert, who sat with a beer stein in his hands, a relic he'd picked up during a vacation to Berlin. Blanche stood behind him with a martini in hand. She leaned behind him, elbows on the back of his chair, eyeing us with an expression that rested somewhere between aggravated and lustful. But, I could have been projecting. In hindsight, it was probably just how she ate her olives that stimulated me to arrive at the conclusion that her eyes were salacious, but I also could be wrong. Because there's nothing more arousing than a woman eating olives from her martini, except, well, I can think of many things.

"Sir," Simon said.

"Hmmm?"

"They asked you a question.

I looked at Simon to clarify, *had I been speaking out loud again?* He nodded as to confirm my suspicions. I hadn't been paying attention one bit.

"Just to clarify," I said, "can you repeat the question?"

"We need this ghost gone," Mr. Mills said. I perked up. *Gone Ghost* sounded like a good movie title. I concluded that I would pocket that for later use in maybe retelling another mystery. Possibly a seventh installment title? I can't think much ahead, generally, because of the alcoholism, but I did feel very proud of myself at that thought, and I chuckled.

"What's funny?" Mills asked.

"A chef slipping on a banana. An old lady honking at a parked car. The words pickle nickels in sequence, but I don't see why any of this is relevant."

"Can you get rid of my ghost or not?" Blanche stepped in. She looked at me directly in the eyes, dropping her de-olived toothpick back in her martini glass and pursing her lips in agitation.

I stood. "I don't take direction very well, and I have no idea what I'm doing, and I do not accept your tone, and I am very confused by the relationship you two have, and I can't stand the way it smells in here, and I don't appreciate how the two-party system at the federal level slows the process of legislative reform to a snail's pace, and YES I'll take the case," I said. And sat in a huff, landing hard on Simon's knee, crossing my arms over my chest like a child getting a bad Christmas present from his grandmother. And though Simon tried to shift me from his lap, I wouldn't allow him. My ego was too damaged.

"Unexpected," Marc said pausing his game for a moment, or losing and having an opportunity to weigh in on the discussion at hand.

"Good," Mr. Mills said, matching my aggravation.

"Why did you tell me that this man, who is clearly alive, was dead?" I said trying to clarify how I was being hired to look into the death of a very alive man.

"Good question," Mr. Mills said.

"I was just about to say that," Simon said.

"I jumped the gun," Blanche said.

"She wishes I were dead," Mr. Mills said. "She's the primary beneficiary on all of my accounts. She'd kill me if she could with her own hands, but..." Mr. Mills put his hand to his lips as if he were concealing his mouth from Blanche but continued speaking at the same decibel level, "... she has a RAP sheet longer than Bruce Springsteen in concert."

"Are you even trying to whisper," I asked. "Also, Bruce Springsteen isn't a rapper."

"Perceptive, sir," Simon said trying to wriggle out from beneath my weight without success.

"Nailed it," Marc said most likely commenting on his getting to the next level in his game.

"Of course, he wanted me to hear. He loves taunting me with his money, but I don't love him for his money. I love him for everything else he provides me," Blanche said kissing the man on the cheek, eyeing me the entire time. As she pulled away, she left lipstick residue on his cheek. I gulped about to comment on her sultry stare, but Simon poked me hard in the side, knowing full well that it was not meant to be acknowledged but merely a tacit stare that would breed discontent in the old man if he knew.

"We'll take the job, but we need accommodations for the weekend, snacks provided, and liquor. A lot of liquor. We prefer pizza for dinner on Saturdays. Dasano's. You can order it or Simon can do it, but the cost of the call will be included in the charges with an extra fee. In addition to the liquor you purchase, we will need full access to your liquor cabinet at all times. If there is a lock on it, we will need ten copies of the key, in case we lose the first nine. We will need at least six highball glasses and silly straws and those little umbrellas that you find in most cocktails. We'll need a constant supply of ice cubes every hour of the day and night. If you do not have an automatic ice dispenser in your fridge, I suggest you start making ice now and continue to do so until the freezer is almost packed."

"Garnish," Marc added, still poking at his phone.

"Yes, and we'll need lemons and oranges. At least a dozen of each if not two, with a potato peeler beside it. My friend here is an expert at flaming the citrus peel, which provides the perfect aromatic twist to these drinks. I'd recommend you both indulge, but that is not part of the stipulations of my employment. If you cannot meet these requirements, we will leave immediately. Otherwise, we can get started now." I looked at my empty glass. "One more refill. We'll get started after that."

Blanche whispered something into Mr. Mills' ear and leaned away. "That can all be arranged," Mr. Mills said. "We'll be back with your drink in a second, and then we can take you on the tour of the house."

"Wonderful," I said.

"If you'll excuse us," Blanche said, as she helped Mr. Mills stand and walked him out of the room towards the kitchen.

"Obvious. She's haunting her own house to kill the old man, man," Marc said.

"I was going to say it's the old man himself trying to get rid of her," Simon said.

"It's a genuine apparition, gentlemen. I know it. I can sense it," I said standing.

"Think about it, Dan. People always call us, and make up some mumbo jumbo about a ghost so you'll come, mess up their house, and accidentally kill somebody," Marc said.

"When has that ever happened?"

"Every single time, bro," Marc said.

"Is that true, Simon?" I asked.

"Approximately 98% of the time, sir," Simon said. "It's usually a false alarm, a lying spouse, an insurance scam."

"And the other two percent?" I asked.

"The haunted maze in Gettysburg, sir. If you'll recall, it was just an elaborate ruse to increase sales, but we got scared and accidentally locked the owner within, as we left, but that was so obviously an accident, and we weren't even called in for questioning. We can chalk the whole thing up to the owner's negligence," Simon said.

"Why would you not put a lock on the inside as well. It's idiotic," I said.

"It was a padlock, sir. He entrusted you with the key, and he did remind you not to lock it as you ran because there was no other way out, and when I reminded you of that, you called me a word I don't think I shall repeat and assured me that he would prefer to stay inside. You said that he would like the challenge," Simon said seeing my counterargument brewing to shift blame to him, but he underestimates. "Also you were drunk."

"You should have used better rhetoric," I said. "You know for certain I have no idea what I'm doing."

"I do, sir. I apologize. I take full responsibility," Simon said.

"So, we have one vote for him. One vote for her. And one vote for ghost," I reminded my colleagues as if somebody could be listening. It's protocol that I tend to utilize reminders in my everyday dialogue. I like to pretend that people I've never met are listening, and thus if they are careless listeners, they can reacclimatize to where I am thoughts. I like to imagine that some scribe somewhere is writing down my every word and publishing my story for readers everywhere to enjoy. If that were the case, this would be the time I would remind them to bet with themselves to see if they can guess the ending based on the story provided up to this point.

So, vote for your favorite ending. Mr. Mills. Blanche. Or ghost. And don't turn to the last page until you read all the way there. That would ruin all the fun.

"Sir," Simon said. "Who are you talking to?"

"Hmm?" I said and looked at where his finger was pointing. It was pointing right in front of my face at a Long Island Iced Tea being held out by Blanche's delicate painted-black fingers. Though in deep thought about her nail color, I took the drink and sucked at the silly straw. Down went the drink in approximately sixteen seconds, and I handed the glass back to Blanche empty. "Now for the tour," I said standing.

Blanche hadn't moved, so we stood nose-to-nose for a moment, staring at one another, much too close for comfort. I could smell her lunch on her breath. The gin only barely shrouded the scent of salsa. She also smelled of cigarettes and a hint of something sour like limeade.

"Follow me," she said. And, we did.

Chapter 7

Textbook haunted houses look like this: rickety wooden staircase leading to a rickety wooden door, broken storm shutters that usually hang by one hinge, at least one boarded-up window, cracked glass somewhere, a big attic with one round window at the center, cracked roofing, and curtains that look like rags. Within, they usually have creaky wooden floors, missing stairs up an enormous staircase, a giant hole in the middle of the floor, huge portraits of old men with carved out eyes so that those who choose to hide behind the wall can peer in on people within, chandeliers that could most likely fall at any moment, rooms with huge beds and fraying canopies, dolls with missing eyes sitting in empty rooms on chairs with missing legs, and a basement that is either locked or strictly off-limits.

This place was exactly the opposite.

Blanche guided us through the house with a warning, "We tore the whole thing down six years ago and rebuilt it from scratch." It was modern, airy, well-lit, and probably going for 2.8 million on Zillown. Not that I look at real estate listings in my off time. I am just a very good judge of Southern California's current real estate market. I often will walk by a property and guess within approximately $100,000 of the property's estimated value. "We had it designed and built by the famous architect, A.R. Bosby. You'll notice that most rooms don't have corners. He was a firm believer in rounding. Even his estimates and quotes tended to be round numbers." She laughed and guided us into the foyer. I didn't. I hate wordplay.

"We entered through here," I said agitated at being on a tour of a space that I had already seen.

"Perceptive, sir," Simon said.

Marc continued playing his game. Not one ounce of Marc gave a hoot about the owl bust over the door.

Blanche looked at me as if she'd taken a bite of a bad apple. "I know," she said, "this is how we get to other rooms." She looked at me through furrowed brow, and I felt uneasy.

"Well," I said to shirk the feeling that she could possibly be judging me for my inane comment, "Get on with it then." It is far better to be condescending to somebody else than to allow them to belittle you. Also, another piece of advice: never admit to saying something stupid. I always retaliate before I can be pinned with embarrassment. "Hashtag waiting," I said, to sound cool and also to be rude simultaneously. I'm pretty certain I nailed it.

"Okay...?" Blanche eyed me, I think finally realizing that I was not downplaying my ineptitude. She continued down two steps that led from the entryway to the dining room, that seemed more for show than function, both the stairs and the room. Who needs two steps to get from room to room, and who needs a dining room when most people eat in their kitchens or living rooms anyway? "This is our dining room. It's usually reserved for special occasions." I was right, as I had grown accustomed to being, "But, you'll see the view is quite nice from the connected balcony."

"Our?" I asked.

"Mine and Stephen's."

"Hmmm," I said as if I understood what that meant, but had trouble reconciling the age gap between the two. Something wasn't really matching up here, but I could neither ask questions nor speak in confidence with Simon so he could give me his opinion on the matter because I felt that it might be rude, but I also knew that I'd probably arrive at an incorrect analysis. From what I was gathering from all of this was that she and Stephen might be intimate, which made me gag audibly. For which, I did not apologize.

The dining room was separated from the balcony by a large tempered glass window. When Blanche flipped a switch, the entire glass partition rose and opened onto the beauty of Griffith Park. A light breeze blew in through the room, wafting in the nasty smell of lavender.

But, the view was so spectacular the scent only bothered my nostrils for a moment before I forgot all about it. I was looking out through the sky, thinking about my apartment, which I shared with the two oafs who held onto my coattails like life-leeches. Disgusting moths attracted to the light of my entrepreneurial endeavors. Two infants suckling on my brilliance, like milk from their mother's teats.

"Sir?" Simon said.

"Hmmm?" I said as I looked back at Simon as to whether I had said any of that out loud, but Simon refused to look at me. I presumed from his silence that he felt embarrassed as byproduct of my rambling. It seemed that he had left me indulging in my own thoughts for too long. And, I had been spewing what I was thinking into the world. I instantly regretted saying such nasty things, but I still refused to apologize. Out of my shame, I stayed in place and waited as they continued on the tour.

They ventured upstairs without me, potentially in a huff, but one that did not make me waver on my opinions.

"I'll be right with you," I said. And then it dawned on me. This haunted house was boring. It felt like it was out of *Country and Town*. Everything was tidy. Everything was clean. Everything was fancy. Where were the cobwebs? Where were the children's toys with missing eyes and missing limbs that had been unused for centuries? Where were the disgruntled cripples hidden away in the nooks and crannies of the abode? Everything in this house was so normal!

I managed to veer away from the tour, citing my IBS as a prime culprit for my sudden disappearance. I had shouted in a calm voice from the bottom of the stairs, "Where's the little boy's room? I need to make a number two."

Blanche responded, "Down the hall and to the left." She also said, "And, please, never say that again. You're a grown man." I found her response quite rude. Obviously, I was not a little boy anymore, and obviously I knew I was a grown man. That was the joke. Yes, I needed to unburden myself, but I thought speaking as though I was but a youth trying to find his way in the halls of an elementary school, an epic quest for the restroom, might be humorous. But, I did not want to call her a buffoon for not understanding, so I let it rest. Instead of following up with them to assure them that I was only kidding before about asking for the lavatory, I went on my own search for the bathroom, not heeding her directions because I was not searching for the lavatory!

In fact, I was searching for the kitchen to assess the liquor situation before following my companions upstairs. I found what I was looking for in an unlocked wooden cabinet. Liquor. The cabinet was painted to look like a vault, a safe from the early 1900s, which I thought was almost too cutesy. But it didn't deter me from mixing my drink. I was able to finally refill my glass in under a minute with a rudimentary Long Island Iced Tea.

I then attempted to accomplish my secondary mission, find a good place to lounge. After... one more refill.

As I finished mixing and drinking my second Long Island Iced Tea, I saw out of my impeccable peripheral vision, a small, almost imperceptible doorway. To the unprofessional eye, it was just sliver of a crack that ran vertically along the entirety of the opposing wall. But, to me, an adept detective with near perfect sight, it stood out like a doorway.

I walked towards it. Something about it screamed *SUSPICIOUS*! As I walked closer, I thought that it could be an entryway, a secret passage, maybe a tunnel to an alternate dimension. I found a handle, curved metal that jutted out from the wall, and I pulled on it. I was correct. It was a door, and maybe it would have been more obvious had I seen the door handle earlier, but I still felt triumphant as I pulled the door open having seen it way before I felt like the average Joe might have.

I opened it and found myself in a room with shelves that lined every wall, filled to the brim with memorabilia. And not just any memorabilia. I could tell by the Swastika insignias on most of the pins, ash trays, jackets, hats, and bands that it was all Nazi memorabilia.

"Are you a history buff, Mr. Marmor?" came a voice from the doorway. I knew the sound was coming from behind me. Having not heard the footsteps, it took me until the verbal recognition to bring myself to turn towards the approaching voice, which was presumably male based on the low tonal quality, maybe an older man based on the gravelly nature of it. As I complete my revolution and finally made eye contact with the person, I found that I was looking at none other than Mr. Mills. A man!

"Aha!" I said, "I suspected it was you by your voice."

"Perceptive, Mr. Marmor," he said.

"It's the low quality of your voice that gave you away," I said.

"Are you interested in," Mr. Mills began but was unable to finish because I had taken over the conversation.

"Women's voices tend to be of a higher pitch, which helped me arrive at my conclusion. So, the voice could only have belonged to four other people, you, Marc, Simon, and myself."

"Very good, Dan. Have you seen," Mr. Mills tried to start again, but I wanted to explain myself further so I didn't let him.

"I knew it could not be me, because I am myself, and I knew that I was not speaking my own name. I knew it was not Marc because he only talks about drinking and women. I knew it was not Simon because he knows I detest history. Therefore, I correctly concluded that the voice must belong to none other than one Mr. Stephen Mills!" I said holding up a Nazi general's sword from one of the shelves with gusto.

Are you not at all interested in World War II?" Mr. Mills said taking the sword from my hand and putting it back on the shelf.

"I find the subject matter, how do I put it, boring," I said picking up what looked like a swastika charm bracelet.

"Have you ever held a *Mein Kampf*?" Mr. Mills said taking the charm bracelet from my hands and putting it back on the shelves.

"I'd rather not," I responded hoping he'd not pull down his pants and expose his kampf to me. I'm not that kind of guy. I averted my eyes.

"No. Have you ever had *Mein Kampf* in your hands? You'd feel its power," he said.

"I don't know what kind of person you think I am, but please keep your kampf to yourself. Is this the kind of thing that happens in every industry in Los Angeles? I had hoped it would be limited to the film industry. But, trust me, Mr. Mills, I will come up with a clever hashtag to expose you if you expose your kampf to me."

"No. The book, Mr. Marmor. *Mein Kampf*."

"You call your erection whatever you'd like. But, I'll tell you it's the first time I've ever heard anybody refer to their penis as a book."

"Mr. Marmor. *Mein Kampf* is a book written by Adolf Hitler." He placed a book in my unwilling hands, and when I finally looked down, I was pleasantly surprised to find that it was not his member after all and just an actual book. It worried me momentarily for his health. A man's Johnson should not be leafy, brittle, and hard-covered. Mr. Mills continued, "That one in your hands is a first edition. I am asking if you've ever seen a book that unique."

"I mostly read books that aren't responsible for genocide."

"It's signed by the man himself." Mr. Mills took the book from me and turned to the front cover. There it was. A short note preceding a signature beneath. I presumed the man himself meant Hitler, the writer, and final solutionist. It was addressed to Heir Stephen Mills.

"Heir Mills? He dedicated this to you?"

"It was signed in 1925," Mr. Mills responded looking at me with confusion.

"You look nothing close to one hundred if you ask me. You've aged well!" I exclaimed.

"It was dedicated to my grandfather, Mr. Marmor."

"Your grandfather would have been very proud of you," I said in a moment of sincerity.

"For what?" Mr. Mills responded with genuine distaste.

"I was going to say for treating an object well for such a long period of time, but actually... Now that I think of it. You're right. Nazis are bad. He might have been disappointed that you kept it."

Disappointed by my answer, he placed the book back on the shelf. "Your father would have been proud of you," he responded.

"For what?" I said miming his response from moments earlier.

"Being an ass." He straightened up. I could feel a tear in my eye, but I tilted my head back in attempt to refrain from crying. He looked at me and saw his mistake. "No. Really. Your father was a good man. He would have liked to see you continuing the family business. Thank you for helping us in our time of need." He put his hand on my shoulder as a way of apologizing.

I instantly straightened up. It was a ruse. I was playing him. For pity! I'd taken an acting class in my formative years, and I had learned a valuable skill of crying on command. Now, I had the power. "Mr. Mills. No need to thank me. It's my job. I do what I am paid for. Not out of generosity and not purely for gratitude. I do it as one performs any service. For money in exchange."

"I'm just saying..."

"Me too." I paused a moment. "Why did Blanche tell me you were dead when you're clearly not? Really."

Mr. Mills balked. "I need to lock up. Let's just call this room off-limits. Okay?" Changing the subject — a classic tactic for somebody who doesn't want to stay on the subject at hand. Various reasons can cause people to change the subject so abruptly, but few cause the subject-changer to look with such wide eyes and a guilty shyness than guilt or secrets.

"Sounds good," I stood stock still, ready for him to leave, hoping he'd stop looking at me with his annoyed eyes. I wanted to continue snooping without interruption. I needed to scour, search, scan, and maybe even sniff out depending on the synonym needed at the time.

"If you left, that would be a lot easier," Mr. Mills said.

I stared at him for a moment longer. He stared back. He wanted me to do something. I could tell. By the way he moved to the side, clearing a pathway for me to the door, and the way he then held his left arm outstretched with palm face up, gesturing towards the door, I knew he was asking me to do something, but I wasn't sure.

After some more detective work, as he continued to eye me, as if I was intruding, maybe that I had maybe overstayed my welcome, that he was feeling uncomfortable or that I had confronted him too directly. I knew then what he wanted me to do. I walked up to him and gave him a big hug, which he didn't reciprocate. Maybe I had deduced wrong.

And, I knew when he said, "Please get out, Mr. Marmor," that I had misconstrued his actions. He'd wanted me to leave the room all along.

Chapter 8

I rejoined the tour upstairs to find the party in the bedroom. Although I had managed to replenish my drink twice, it was already empty before I made it upstairs. Luckily, I knew Marc had the emergency thermos in his camera bag. He snapped candid photos of Blanche as she smoked cigarettes on the balcony. They stood by the fire pit, gazing into the backyard, which was filled with a variety of cacti and stones. I watched them look over the horizon and thought to myself, *what did I miss?*

"Not much," Blanche said casually, still smoking her cigarette.

I looked at Simon, who was reading on the couch; he looked back at me and shrugged, assuming that I knew what had transpired based on her verbal reaction, but I didn't. I raised my eyebrow and gestured for him to explain further, though wordlessly. And, he nodded, which I took to mean that I had said it aloud. He resumed reading, continuing *Paradise Lost*. Still unable to grasp his gestures, I said, "Did I say that out loud?"

"You did, sir," he said and flipped the page with a callous movement, almost an aggravated punctuation mark.

"Yeah, man. You did," Marc said pouring me another drink as I unconsciously held my glass outwards towards him, more of an instinctive measure by now, more of an autonomous motion than an acutely aware one.

"We see him out there sometimes," Blanche said. "Aimlessly wandering. Sometimes it kicks over a rock, or unearths a cactus. It's frustrating to say the least," Blanche said.

"Whose place is this?" I asked astutely. I can be quite the questioner if the time comes about.

"Ours."

"Ours? I assure you. We, you and I, do not live here together. First, my apartment is approximately a quarter of the size of the bed you sleep on. And, two..."

"Second, sir," Simon said.

"Second," I continued, "You and I just met not six hours ago. Refill me, Marc."

"A please would be nice," Marc said coolly.

"Yes, it would," I responded. He poured my drink, and I could tell by the way no liquor filled my glass that he was out.

"Can we have the room?" Blanche said as if to nobody, focusing purely on the grounds below.

"Absolutely. I'll brew a new batch of Marc's famous Long Island Iced Tea, or Marc will. I'm far from a mixologist and even farther from patient," I said turning towards the door, snapping for Marc and Simon to follow.

"I meant you and me, Mr. Marmor."

"Obviously," I said turning again, and snapping my fingers for Simon and Marc to continue their trek towards the door. They left, and I was alone looking into Blanche's big black eyes. She walked towards me, with her hips swaying, her lips slightly spread.

She stood right in front of me and stopped. We stared at one another for a long while. Longer than I felt really comfortable doing.

I couldn't tell if she was going to speak or kiss me so I let her know that, "I can't tell if you're going to talk to me or kiss me, but I will warn you that I don't kiss clients, and this is far too close for comfort in terms of speaking."

And, in that moment, I could tell that she was brazenly beautiful, and I don't just say that for alliterative purposes. I say that because she was bewitchingly brilliant with her big beaming breasts and breakneck backhand. I only say breakneck backhand because she smacked me so hard I saw sideways with the back of her hand. Well, my face turned to the side after she hit me, and thus I saw sideways. Therefore, her breakneck backhand made me see sideways.

When I turned back, she was already kissing me. Her lips engaged with mine, her tongue slip-sliding its way into my mouth. It felt slimy. She held the back of my head with her long fingers as she held my face to hers. I couldn't help but wonder if she had a virus of any kind and was infecting me with her saliva.

She pulled away from me as if shocked by some kind of static friction, some sensation that made her stop sucking on my face. "You are the rudest man I've evet met," she said. "I cannot believe you just said that."

"What?" I said, and looked for Simon to corroborate whether or not I had spoken aloud, but I'll be damned if he wasn't in the room. That sidekick of mine was always scampering away for one reason or another. Six months ago, he needed to visit his mother in the hospital while I was on a routine scouting operation. The year before that, he had pancreatic cancer and had to go to chemotherapy while I was on the biggest ghost hunt of my life. Three years before that, he'd been involved in a car accident, in a car that I'd been driving and he couldn't come to my bedside to help me drink my apple juice and eat my apple sauce. Neglectful. Barely even a friend.

She smacked me again. Harder this time. I could feel the tingling sensation in my face. "You need to learn to keep your mouth shut."

"First, I need not learn anything, my dear. It tires out the brain. Also…"

"Second," Blanche said.

"I'm glad you agree, but I'm in the middle of a sentiment here, my dear Blanche. Also, if I kept my mouth shut, the kissing wouldn't be as enjoyable."

"You idiot," she said.

"I must remind you that I clearly have no idea what I'm... " I couldn't finish my thought. Her tongue was already probing my mouth again, kissing me deeply, passionately.

"I'm sure your husband would not be pleased by your promiscuous behavior," I said in garbled vowels and consonants for, you see, it is quite difficult to speak when there is a tongue shoved deep into your oral cavity.

"What?" she asked annoyed.

"I'm sure your husband would not be pleased by your promiscuous behavior," I repeated.

"He's not my husband. Stephen is a friend. A good friend," she said. Her tone implied sensuality, a kind of lustful reminiscence occurring in her mind.

"But he's your lover."

"Perceptive, Mr. Marmor."

"Really?" I said both stunned by my own deductive ability and by the mental image of Blanche and Mr. Mills engaging in erotic behavior. That's when it hit me. If she had kissed Mr. Mills, or worse, she couldn't possibly have used any other tongue to kiss me just a moment earlier.

My disgust must have been apparent in my scowl because she explained, "We have an arrangement."

"I don't need to get personal with you. We are in the midst of a professional relationship, one that has already been breached by our swapping spit. Pardon my French and my French kissing. I've barely been intimate before besides that time I kissed the neighbor's precocious dog, made love to my gym sock, which I've had long and steady relations with, and the occasions I practiced on a kissing pillow that I purchased from Amazoon for $12.99 with free shipping due to the Amazoon Pryme account I siphoned from Simon along with his Netflicks, Chulu, and UTube Red accounts. I also have his Blockbooster Video card, which hasn't been useful for a long time."

"I'm going to level with you, Mr. Marmor."

"Dan. Call me Dan."

"No," she said. "Mr. Marmor, I'm a flame. I'm burning for life, adventure, feeling." She squeezed my thigh with her hand, very hard. Uncomfortably hard. "I'm being extinguished, Mr. Marmor. Everyday I'm with that man, my fire dies. I need to be ignited. I need to burn. I need to be ablaze. Spark me, Mr. Marmor. Ignite me, Mr. Marmor. Light me, Mr. Marmor." Her hand slowly traced up my inner thigh.

"I'll get it out for you," I said, reaching into my pocket to take out my Zipo lighter, which I had brought just in case she needed it at a moment like this. I instantly flicked the spark wheel, and the flint burst into flames.

She bit at the inside of her lip. Thought of it a moment and then took from her purse another cigarette. She put it to her lips.

"Stephen doesn't like when I smoke inside. Will you join me on the balcony?"

"I will, but I won't."

"Excuse me."

"Ambiguous phrasing. I will join you on the balcony, but I will not join you in smoking. I try to refrain from tainting my lungs. Bad for longevity. In short, it'll kill you."

"Do you ever shut up?"

"Often. Primarily when I'm sleeping, but also when I'm inhaling, listening, and eating. Also drinking. It's hard to drink when speaking, but I can assure you I know that only because of trial and error."

"Just shut up," she said gripping my lips betwixt her thumb and index finger and pulled me towards the balcony.

"The customer's always right," I managed to say through the corners of my mouth.

Chapter 9

As we walked on the balcony, she clapped her hands together. A fire instantly rose from the pit they had set up in the middle of the balcony, and light jazz played from the speakers overhead. She smiled at me. "Do you dance?" she said.

"I do," I said. "Not," I finished. A joke I'd learned in third grade but which, like me, hadn't gotten old.

She took my hand in hers, and she slowly guided me in a light tango. I'd never attempted a tango. I don't dance. I have never danced. I don't like to dance. I don't want to dance. I have never tried to dance. I am not good at dancing.

"It's easy," she said.

We swirled and twirled anyway, and by God's delicious cheesecake, I started to enjoy it. Invigoration surged through my loins, and I took the lead, which I certainly know nothing about, and I spun Blanche. I spun, and I spun, and I spun. I was delighted. I was having fun. I'd never danced like that before, and it felt fantastic. Her feet lifted off of the floor, as I twirled around and around. It must have felt strange because she giggled, "Put me down."

I laughed, thinking that she was taken by the spirit, too. I felt her warmth, and I looked into her eyes. I could see the electric dust particles that form in the eye from lack of oxygen to the brain. I felt an uneasiness in my stomach, like nausea. I felt dizzy. I felt her weightlessness in my arms as her legs lifted, like she was levitating in my grasp, the beautiful, magnificent woman who had somehow stolen my fancy. Forbidden fruit. To covet a man's wife. But they aren't married. She said that. Right? For a moment, I thought, *is this what love feels like?* I smiled. *Could this be the feeling my mother had told me about? Could this be the feeling Ms. Oldstein taught me about in Sexual Education? Could she be the birds to my bees?*

Blanche eyed me. I tried to look beyond her for Simon to verify my suspicion that I'd said these thoughts out loud, but he still wasn't there.

That's when it happened.

The apparition appeared. It blew through the balcony and out the fire. I gasped as the song buffered, the modern-day equivalent of a record skipping, and I let go of Blanche mid-step as I scanned for the ghost, unable to see it with my naked eye.

"I think it's here," I said to Blanche as I gazed upon the now flameless fire-pit, but she was no longer there. *Huh*, I thought. *Where'd she go?* I looked around the balcony, and there I found her. Over the edge, in her beautiful garden, in a bloody heap, tangled within a nest of cacti.

"What are you doing down there?" I shouted.

She groaned in response. Not the conversational gymnast she thought she was.

Chapter 9a (Simon's Section)

Good morning, afternoon, evening or night, readers all! I do not mean to jolt you from your peaceful reading session with direct address, however, Mr. Marmor has asked me to write this section from my point of view; I have discussed with him a significant moment he has described in the previous chapter. I was on the floor below and therefore saw the incident from a different angle. Mr. Marmor asked that I write my thoughts down, though I'm not a wordsmith, not by inclination or by trade. He has told me that I feature prominently in the pages previous, but he has not let me read them for fear that my criticism might tamper with the future story elements as he feels that he has already set forth the arc in the previous pages. For this, I applaud his endeavors and his artistic take on the matter. I will do my best to adhere to the highest literary standards.

I have, as I am certain you do not know, read *Paradise Lost* several times.

I hope not to bore you. I will keep my writing brief, for as the great Bard said, "Brevity is the soul of wit." I hope to be witty, charming, and true to the story.

You must first let me explain who I am.

Simon Sidwell at your service. I am, at the moment of writing this, aged thirty-six. Mr. Marmor thinks I am younger. I don't know why. Maybe, he presumes my small stature, small voice, and shy nature be indicative of a youthful disposition. Yet, he has neither asked me of my age nor has he asked me of any other personal matter. I can only imagine that his brain must be too busy with other thoughts to deal with the pleasantries of dialogue's due diligence. I am originally from Croydon, born and raised on Colson Road, just south of London proper. My mum was a firebrand. She could crack a joke or a skull in one shake of a broomstick. My father was a debt-collector, went off one day to collect a debt and never returned.

I attended Cambridge University, where I read computer science and engineering. I developed programs used in crypto-currency transactions in the early 2000s. I made my first few million immediately after graduation.

I must pause here to ask you: Please, do not tell Mr. Marmor of my financial well-being. I've found that he often will pretend to be out of money while in line at fast food restaurants so I will offer to pay for him, but I always have some kind of excuse, my supposed poverty being my primary rationale. Thinking me a pauper from the streets of London, constantly mocking me with a Cockney accent (though I do not have one), Dan usually gives up on the fast food and heads to a local convenience store where he steals himself a cup of Ramen Noodles and fills it up at the hot-water tap provided by said bodega at the tea and coffee station. He eats it as he browses the contents of the convenience store's shelves. Dan feels quick-witted and bright when he completes his subtle pick-pocketing routine and quickly shoves the scalding hot noodles into his mouth, like he's pulled one over on the suckers of big business. Little does he know, I pay for it every time, without his knowledge of course, before we leave. Luckily, it's only one dollar than the ten or more he might spend on fast food if I ever offered to pay his fare.

After university, I developed hardware to detect electromagnetic impulses and radiation. My goal was to understand the natural and unnatural worlds. I hoped to explore dimensions unknown. I built quantum analyzers, proton rays, alpha wave generators, ectoplasmic resisters, and even state-of-the-art gas grills.

Dan and I met one day while I was on holiday in New York City. I had just seen a performance of *Kats* (the musical) on a ticket I had purchased when I found out Nicole Sherzinger would be playing the role of Grizybella. I was extremely disappointed when I received notice the day of the performance that she had been replaced by Lena Lewis. The Voice had invited Sharzinger to be a judge. I left the theater feeling gypped, as though the Big Apple had a pulled a good old-fashioned Charlie Chaplin on me. I stopped at a local pub for a cider, a vice in which I sometimes indulge. I found Dan standing atop a stool, giving a toast at the top of his lungs though nobody listened. I remember it being a rousing and intelligent speech. I applauded his golden tongue and helped him down from the chair. He smelled of gin and belched as he sat.

We talked philosophy and religion and politics and spirituality, and he kept ordering round after round. Six days later I came out of my drunken stupor in a tuk-tuk in downtown Phuket, searching for a wraith that Dan had said was just right around the corner.

We've been friends and colleagues ever since. It pleases me that he feels I am his sidekick because it offers me cover: my infamy in London after I singlehandedly flash-crashed the crypto-market when I sold all of my holdings put a solid target on my head in London's underground circles.

I have travelled with Dan ever since, fighting ghastly crimes, starting my long tenure in Dan Marmor's newly minted Mystery Box.

On the day in question, Dan had asked that I attend Marc in the kitchen and make some more of his favorite concoctions though I had been sober for over two years and often pretended to drink along with him. Dan has what I suppose some might call a problem. In my adventures with him so far, I have come down with a severe case of Type 2 diabetes and an even worse case of alcoholism, both of which have gotten under control since I went cold turkey. My new sobriety does make Dan slightly intolerable, but I would never complain about my employer. Except on occasions when he becomes quite the tosser.

But I shall be briefer. I was in the kitchen with Marc, admiring the silver. Elegant. All the same. Unlike our utensil drawer. I would liken it to a bargain bin at a thrift store, a wild array of individually styled pieces most likely found in trash bins or at garage sales for ten cents apiece.

We were in the kitchen, which has a splendid view of the backyard, and I was taking in the scene as Marc used the extensive armory of shakers and mixers to create what he called the Montauk of all Long Island Iced Teas. I abhor them for the sneaky way they slip past the taste buds with their sweetness only to pack a punch so strong they can knock a man on his fanny, in the American sense of the word. I could smell the liquor waft through the air as I gazed gaily upon the pleasant view of the cactus patch.

If you've ever heard the song, "It's Raining Men," you might understand the next moment better. Except imagine the song instead were called, "It's Raining Women!" For that's what followed. A woman, more specifically Blanche, fell from the sky as if she were a singular, giant raindrop, her arms and legs flailing, like rubber sticks from her body, spinning like a frisbee, splayed out as she flew out into the backyard from the first story balcony to the ground floor. It happened so fast, it didn't register all at once.

Her long, black flowing hair trailed her as she sailed towards the ground, pulled forcefully by gravity's unforgiving constancy. She landed noiselessly as the ice in Marc's shaker audibly overtook the landing, which was ungraceful to say the least. She landed atop a cactus patch, her body twisting unnaturally as each of her extremities caught on different pokers.

Still, she looked ravishing if you were to ask me. A beauty.

And I'm fairly certain that is that. If more comes to mind I shall ask Dan for more input on further chapters. Thank you for your attention, dearest of readers, up until this point, and I do hope you enjoy the rest of this story.

Chapter 9b (Marc's Section)

Literally no idea what this guy wants. Dan handed me three sheets of loose-leaf, thinking it only fair that I get my own section if Simon gets his. But, I have nothing to add. Except this. I guess.

Long Island Iced Tea Recipe:

Mix one part vodka, one part rum, one part gin, one part tequila one part triple sec, and two parts sweet and sour mix.

Use a shaker to mix furiously with ice. Add some egg white if you want some good head. And serve chilled in a hurricane glass with a splash of cola and a lemon slice as garnish.

If you drink it, and it doesn't taste like a teenage girl's breath at a Bieber concert, you're doing it wrong. Dan likes it because it gets him wasted, and I don't mind a healthy buzz either so… yeah. That's it.

Chapter 10

Six broken ribs. A broken tibia. Clavicle snapped perfectly in two, breaking skin, both splintered edges pointing upwards. Right arm broken in fifteen different places. Concussion. Mild aphasia. And stitches galore.

It took medics two and a half hours to peel her body from the cacti's clutches, and another two hours to rip each thorn from her beautiful body.

Mr. Mills was equally shocked that the ghost had thrown her from the balcony. I didn't tell him we had been dancing because I felt as though it might inspire jealous feelings, and since he was to be my employer for the next few days I didn't want to breed a rivalry. Also, it could be construed as my fault for carelessly flinging her from the balcony. I didn't feel the need to explain my innocence. It might complicate the issue. So I kept the whole thing to myself. Believing that the incident had been caused by a ghost also gave Mr. Mills more incentive to keep my team and me around. For if it were perceived as the ghost's doing, my presence on the property might prove a necessity.

And I was in dire need of consistent employment, as my coffers seemed to be emptying on their own. My bar tabs themselves were exorbitant, an issue I might need to investigate in a later episode. Surely a demon's doing.

I apologize for my absence in the previous two chapters. I thought it might be beneficial to my cause to have eye witnesses weigh in on Blanche's fall. I just wanted to verify my innocence just in case the issue was ever revisited in the United States court system.

As they took the unconscious and heavily sedated Blanche facedown into the ambulance, Mr. Mills gave us the full go ahead to start our investigations as he tended to Blanche at the hospital.

And this was my time to shine! This is the moment I lived for. I emptied my box on the floor of the living room and gathered our goods. It was time to find that damned ghost.

"It's time to find this damned ghost! " I shouted, raising my fists triumphantly.

"You just said that, sir," Simon said.

"Twice. First time you kinda muttered it," Marc added.

"I must really mean it then," I said, and hoped the agitation wasn't coming through in my tone.

I strapped on my Camelpak, which Simon had so graciously donated to the cause a few years ago. It was a slim fitting hydration backpack I had modified. I filled all thirty-six ounces of the plastic inner-container with Marc's wondrous cocktail, his Long Island Iced Tea. And that would sustain me for at least fifteen minutes, largely because the artificial nipple that led to the bladder in the backpack was hard to guzzle from. If you tried really hard you could get only a steady drip.

The preliminary round of searching gave us nothing. It was still daylight, and the readings all turned up null. I sprayed endo-serum on all the corners of every room, which somehow bleached the polished wood floors. I lit sage in the center of every room and accidentally set off the fire alarm twice, which coated everything in a slimy, watery film. And while sticking the carbon-fiber, illuminated lens down each pipe, I accidentally knocked over an entire shelving unit of vintage wine, breaking over two hundred bottles of red and white on the basement floor. All attempts to get the attention of this apparition proved unsuccessful.

Night had fallen over the expansive west coast and our first round of inspection was completely fruitless, aside from the added bottles of liquor we found in the basement and used to refill my Camelpak.

Ultimately, we all wound up lounging in the comfort of the huge couch in the living room watching *Angry Girls* on the plasma screen TV while eating hummus and pretzel crackers and drinking Long Island Iced Teas. I can tell you for those few hours, I could not have been happier with how the ghost hunt was turning out.

Though we didn't find any ghosts, we did have an amazing slumber party kind of night. We watched television and ate until we had indigestion. We laughed with Lindsay Lohan every step of her hilarious high school journey. It was a night filled with complete and untampered glee. I can't remember a time I ever laughed more. We ate popcorn and gossiped about old crushes, and we drank. Boy, did we drink. We drank, and we drank, and we drank.

Come midnight, Mr. Mills returned, exhausted both emotionally and physically after a day with Blanche in the hospital — only to find us playing Twisster in his living room.

I swore that it was part of our ghost-hunting routine, one that was sacred on the first night of any good scout, but I'm afraid my speech was so slurred that he merely threw up his hands, giving up without so much as a good night. He lumbered upstairs.

Soon after he left, he returned to counsel us on the tinnitus-inducing effects of loud music on the ear drums.

"What?" I said.

He responded, "Turn down the music, and I'm sure you'll be able to hear me."

"What?" I responded again, though I had heard every word he said.

"Turn it down, will ya? I'm trying to sleep!"

Between the Buried and Me played loudly on Mr. Mills' speaker system. It's technical death metal that slips in and out of genre, sneaking in some classical, jazz, and sea shanties during the interludes. The album, "Color," took us through its winding graces as we listened as loudly as the system would possibly go. I knew what Mr. Mills was telling us to do, but I used the same tactics I'd used on Bobby the landlord to continue playing it for as long as possible.

"Turn it off," Mr. Mills shouted loudly, his bathrobe opening to reveal dirty tighty-whities underneath.

"This is how we always listen to our music. Always have. Always will. It helps flush out the ghosts." I presume he again didn't understand a word of it because he looked dumbly at me as if I were speaking in tongues and returned to his chamber.

"Let's give him some music he might enjoy," I shouted to Simon who was already on top of it.

We finished Twisster as Shanya Twain belted out her final verses of "These Boots Were Made for Walking." My eyes could no longer stay open then. I collapsed on the spot with right hand red, left foot blue, left hand yellow, and right food green and fell into a deep and restful slumber.

Chapter 11

I awoke the next morning to sunshine shining directly into my eyes. It burned like the flames of a thousand suns. Not even just a thousand, a million. Like hellfire, my brain struck six chords at once, all discordant, all reigning with supreme vengeance upon my delicate psyche. My stomach battled against itself as nausea slowly swept through my gut like an acidic monsoon.

His voice rang through the house like Satan calling Cerberus. "Mr. Marmor!" the demonic vessel shouted.

It wasn't Satan, though. It was Mr. Mills. He stood over me, and I tried to wriggle my way into the shade he created, but he put his foot atop my head and stood there. "In my office. Now!" He stared down at me as I gawked up and him, the contents of my stomach boiling up into my esophagus. Like a tea kettle boiling over, I could almost hear the sound of my brain hissing out of my ears with a high-pitched whistle, and then the noise stopped. The pot had boiled over, and without being able to hold it back, I vomited on Mr. Mills' shoes.

"You. In my office. Now!" he shouted again and walked off, releasing an annoyed sigh.

"Me?" I belched back, wiping my mouth with the back of my hand.

But Mr. Mills, so rudely, did not respond. He simply turned and walked from the room as if he expected me to follow, like I was some kind of lackey, some kind of paid Collie, there to lick his wounds, and help him solve *his* crises. Little did he know I had my own issues to solve.

"Me?" I asked Simon who sat stunned at the table reviewing the readings from the previous night.

"I believe so, sir," Simon said. Apparently, he had been trying to get me up for the last twelve hours. It was already afternoon, I presumed by the daytime TV that was droning in front of a passed-out Marc.

My head lolled on the shoulders that were there to support the neck that seemed to collapse in on itself as I stood. I pulled myself up from the floor using the leg of the glass table to stand, untangled myself from the Twister board that had curled around me like a boa constrictor, and balanced on the shifting ground that swayed beneath my feet. I braved the Earth's current, a captain bracing himself on the bow of a ship called Earth that raced through the cosmos, bouncing and bopping from star to star as we crashed through the oceanic tides of the universe.

I walked, or stumbled, or collapsed into his office shortly thereafter. Man overboard.

Mr. Mills sat across from me with dead eyes, his hands folded neatly on his lap, his lips pursed tightly together, his gray hair combed over his balding crown, and his aviator glasses hanging loosely from his shirt. His furrowed brow, his wrinkled nose, and his loud exhalations did little to define his emotions. To me, they looked like they were somewhere between contemplative and content. But it was a red herring all along. I knew what his emotional state was when he said, "I'm angry," that in fact he was contemptuous. "I am mad, irate, and quite frankly, Mr. Marmor, pissed right off."

"That sounds like a medical problem to me. Out of my wheelhouse, but I can ask Simon. Maybe he has something in his satchel that can help you to reattach it."

"No, you imbecile. My house. My collectibles. My floor. My carpets. My furniture. My iPad! All ruined. And Blanche! My poor Blanche. She's a wreck."

"Don't talk about her like that. She looks as though she's quite well-off. I wouldn't even venture to guess her monthly income. So, I'd appreciate you only referring to Blanche with pleasant terms from this point forward. It's rude, after all, to call women names without them in your presence."

"It's rude to call women names always," he responded.

"I'm glad we agree on the matter."

"We agree on nothing, Mr. Marmor," he said. "You are being completely and utterly impossible."

"Rude. I'm here to find the ghost, not to teach you manners. May I get back to work?" I stood trying to end the conversation.

But then Mr. Mills stood and slammed his fist on the desk. He was about to speak. I could see his lip quivering and his inhaling, preparing to speak. I sat.

I realized that he could be considering rescinding his offer of employment, so I changed my tact. "Mr. Mills," I said. A display of courtesy, a display of respect, a display of propriety. I'm not one to apologize, but I believe in respecting elders, respecting rights of others, and respecting the great flag of the United States of America!" I put my hand to my heart and felt oddly patriotic for a moment.

"Go, but don't mess anything else up, or you're out of here with no pay," I had appeased the beast. Mr. Mills sat again. As he sat, I stood. Almost like a see-saw. The thought reminded me of how uneasy the ground was, and how we were constantly floating through space. I was ready to retort with some quip or putdown or witty repartee, but instead, the pH balance of my belly had me racing to the nearest restroom, and I'll tell you in a big house like that, without having paid attention on the tour, I didn't make it in time.

Chapter 12

"Because of your antics, the two of you," I scolded Marc and Simon, "we are in a tentative employment situation, one that requires our utmost scrutiny and attention to detail. I'd recommend you both shape up and fly right. Otherwise, it's out on the street for you bums with no pay!"

"You're not paying us anyway," Marc said.

"I'm not?" I asked.

"No, sir," Simon said. "You said that we were doing this pro bono, sir."

"I did?" I asked. "I did!" I said. "Of course, I did."

Marc poured himself and then me a new drink.

"I was scouring the readings last night, sir," Simon said, "And, I found something quite fishy. There was seismic activity from 3 AM to 5 AM despite no reported earthquake. Though all other readings turned up negative, I think the seismic activity could be due to the presence of a gh— "

"Do I look like an imbecile?" I interrupted. "Mr. Mills called me an imbecile, and it hurt my feelings. It seemed quite rude too as I was reprimanding him for his verbal abuse of his infirmed woman-friend. So, I ask... do I look like an imbecile?"

"You look awful," Marc said.

I looked to Simon to see if this was the truth. I felt awful, and I was worried that it might be true. Simon shrugged in the affirmative.

"You're right. I should freshen up. I'll use the whirlpool tub in the master bathroom."

"I wouldn't do that if I were you, sir. The readings are coming from that area of the house, sir," Simon said.

But, I was sick of listening to Simon speak. So, I left and headed for the master bathroom to rinse off the filth that was still toxic in my system. Maybe a give myself a nice shave, and a light steam if I could get my head around the processes associated with my morning bathroom rituals, despite the hellish hangover that was still clouding my judgement.

One more drink for the road, and maybe I'd be back on my game, I thought. "The hair of the dog," I said.

"That's not how it works, sir" Simon said.

"Huh?" I asked casually.

"Nothing, sir," Simon said.

"Mhmm." I wasn't listening.

"You're not listening. Am I right, sir?"

"Mhhmm," I said, still not listening, downing another full glass of Long Island Iced Tea as I went to the bathroom.

Chapter 13

The bathroom was like no bathroom I'd ever seen before. I had heard talk of the whirlpool from Marc who imagined the night before how it must feel to bathe a rich man. He clarified after some razzing that he had meant bathing as a rich man instead of helping a rich man bathe, which I thought was quite odd for him to say considering how lustful he is towards the opposite sex.

A lot of what Marc had focused on was the bathroom specifications. A whirlpool was his number one draft pick for his ideal commode. In my ideal bathroom, my primary concern would be two-ply toilet paper. It's been years since I have felt the warm and gentle caress of Charmin between my bare cheeks. The luxuries of the one percent. I guess I will never indulge in the wonders of that bear-approved bottom brusher. For now, I find solace knowing that I will continue to, in my ascetic lifestyle, use single-ply toilet paper akin to Brillo pads, to which I've grown quite accustomed.

The room is large, the space white, not a speck of dust anywhere on any surface. They must have maids. Real maids. That clean. Like really clean. Like dust and vacuum, the works. Along the walls, there were five doors leading to different chambers, with two small steps leading to each. Behind door one, the whirlpool. Behind door two, the steam bath. Behind door three, the sauna. Behind door four, the shower, and behind door five, a bunch of towels. Now, the wondrous part rests in the center of the room.

There was a cross section of three-foot-high walls meeting like an X in the perfect center of the room with black lines on the floor daggering out to show the four separate sections of the bathroom's facilities. In one quadrant of this four-part bathroom sectional, there was the toilet, a beautiful porcelain TOTO machine with heated seat, automatic toilet paper dispenser, shag bathmat, motion-sensor flusher, and a pull-out table for a laptop to sit on. In the neighboring quadrant, a bidet, gilded, with flor-de-lis etched into the wall. In the other two sections, two separate sinks with hanging mirrors for each user. A His and a Hers.

I urinated in one of the sinks, not wanting to disturb the high-tech toilet seat. Mr. Mills had told me not to mess anything up, and I think his words played over and over in my head as I turned on the faucet to wash away the vile scent of 80-proof urine.

The layout didn't make sense to me at first, but then I looked up. The ceiling was one spotless, speckless, pristine mirror! I looked up, and the floorplan finally made sense to me. I was standing in one section of an aerial view of a bathroom-based swastika! The vertical walls the equal arms of the center, and the black etchings on the floor, the right angled ninety-degree extensions of the swastika's arms.

I didn't want to jump to conclusions, but I was starting to think that based on the room filled with Nazi memorabilia and this bathroom, I thought it safe to deduce that Mr. Mills might be a real live, modern, educated history major.

Though maybe in a past life I would have let it bother me, I wouldn't let his success despite his useless liberal arts degree affect me. I threw on the faucet to the whirlpool and let the tub fill with water. It took a while. Unaccustomed to baths, I hummed the theme song to *Duck Tales*, a song that continually gets stuck in my head and buzzes around my skull like a trapped bee, stinging my lips into action during moments of serenity. I hummed as I poured soap into the tub and released a bath bomb that I found in the cupboard above the tub. A bath bomb, I'd learned from the label on the side, was the next level in bubble baths and not a legitimate weapon designated for unsuspecting bathers.

I had run through the song about twenty times before the entire tub had filled. I had gotten so involved in the tune and in trying to hit perfect pitch for each note, that I only stopped the flowing water when the tub had already overflowed and was spilling onto the floor around me and the bubbles were already towering high above the lip of the porcelain.

I stripped out of my clothing, hung my wardrobe from the hook, and dunked myself in the tub, spilling more water onto the already drenched floor. I lowered myself farther into the tub, pained by how hot the water was, but I knew that it would cool down sooner than I hoped, so I braved the heat to enjoy the tub for longer.

Letting out an involuntary groan of satisfaction, I fully immersed myself in the tub. And, when I reemerged, I felt a presence.

Between my feet, as if rising from the drain, the bubbles from my bath bomb began to form into a creature. It gurgled and belched. All of a sudden, this thing, an amalgamation of all of the hair and lint and dead skin and dirt trapped in the drain, all backed up at once into a human form that rose before me, the Bubbleman. Like the Boogeyman but made entirely of bubbles. And it smelled like sickness, like bile, like death.

I held my breath, not that I didn't want to breathe, just that my gasp got stuck in my chest with terror. Eight arms of bubbles extended slowly from the ascending bubble-mass, almost spider-like, and one large bubble started to grow from the top of the bubble thing that stood before me, like one large bubble-head. And, that bubble grew bubbles for eyes, thousands of them like a fly's. It then grew a bubble for a nose, and two long bubbles for a mouth, and even more bubbles for a frizzy hair-do. This Bubbleman opened its bubble mouth to reveal its sharp bubble teeth and said, "GET OUT OF THIS HOUSE, HEATHEN!"

I tried to push myself back, to climb from the tub, but I found that it was too slippery. It proved impossible to climb from, and all around me the walls of the tub rose high, and I felt as though I was turning into the size of a mouse as I clawed and clawed against the bottom of the tub uselessly.

The ghost bellowed an insidious laugh. It said, "I'M GOING TO GET YOU, DANNY. I'M GOING TO KILL YOU, DANNY! YOU AND YOUR ENTIRE FUCKING MYSTERY TEAM, DANNY. YOU AND EVERYBODY YOU LOVE, DANNY. EVERYTHING IN YOUR LIFE, DANNY. I'M GOING TO TAKE IT, DANNY, AND I'M GOING TO MURDER IT, DANNY. YOU HEAR

THAT?" The figure lifted its feet and stomped on the tub behind me. It leaned in and whispered with frothy fumes, "You hear it?" He stomped again. "That's the sound that your little head is going to make when I smash it to pieces, Danny." The bubbles popped and popped as it shook over me, dripping soapy, sudsy water on my already wet body.

"Now, get DER ARSCH out of here before I drown you with my big, bubble SCHWANZ, DANNY!" And as the figure cackled behind me, I turned and looked up at it. Its face directly in front of mine, the thing burped bubbles, which floated just above my head, and suddenly the entity collapsed.

The bubbles popped and soaked me in its filthy bubble-guts. And the tub emptied as it disappeared, swirling down the drain like it was caught in a vortex. The jets whirred against nothing as I sat in the tub, gripping my knees, terrified by what had just happened. When I finally opened my eyes to see that the being was gone, I ran for the door, screaming and slipping and sliding my way to the door like a clumsy and horrified figure skater on the soapy floor. There were bubbles everywhere. Six inches deep of thick, dark bubbles.

I opened the door and saw that bubbles had leaked their way under the onto the carpet, soaking the already slimy carpet in grimy juices of the sewage system. I sloshed through soggy shag until I got back to the living room, and like a frightened child stuttering through a ghost story, I ran into the room and shouted, "I s-s-s-saw a g-g-g-g-g-."

"You're stuttering, sir," Simon said.

"And you're naked," Marc finished.

"A g-g-g-g-g—g-g-g-ghost!" I finally spit out. Just then, I heard something bump behind me, a squeaky squeak like rusted metal. From the sound of it, I could tell it wasn't footsteps of any human. It was too mechanical, too sharp, too high-pitched. It had to be something else, a mechanical monster, an AI artifice, a gear-grinding goblin, a robotic wraith, but I couldn't be sure until I looked. Innately too terrified to stay still, I jumped into Simon's arms and finally caught a glimpse of the being that broke the silence behind me. I was right! It wasn't just a human.

Covered in bandages and braces and casts and stitches galore. Two black eyes and her head done up in white gauze, a neck brace, and her left leg sticking out in a cast, I knew then exactly what it was. It was Blanche in a wheelchair!

"Hello, Mr. Marmor," Blanche said, "You're back."

Involuntarily, as I had jumped into Simon's arms, I let a sound erupt from my mouth, something I'd never heard come out of me before, something squeakier than a toy horn and louder than a car horn and wimpier than a baby bjorn and visceral, like paper being torn. I let out a shriek that only a teenage girl could make at a boy band concert, something that made me embarrassed as it left my body, and it lasted longer than I'd have hoped, longer than my realization that she wasn't a monster lasted. My scream continued on and on and on.

Even while Blanche gawked at me, annoyed, and Simon let me fall to the ground to cover his ears, and Marc left the room, I continued to squeal in terror.

Marc came back with a drink for me, and when he put the drink in my hand, I continued to shriek. But, the alluring scent of the cocktail wafted into my nose, so I stopped briefly, chugged the drink down to the bitters at the bottom, letting the ice hit my lips so I could get out every last drop, and then... I continued screaming while holding the empty glass out for Marc to refill, which he promptly did.

As soon as the glass was filled, I stopped momentarily to take another drink, took a nice long swig, and then let the epic wail again from my esophagus that I just couldn't keep down until...

I said, "Oh. Hi, Blanche!" and then kept screaming and screaming and screaming for another thirty minutes at least.

Chapter 14

We sat in Mr. Mills' office, which looked more like a crypt than a study. He had his fingers intertwined, his aviators atop his head, pulling back his long gray hair. Blanche sat beside him. Her left leg was her only extremity uninjured in the fall. Because of the cast on her other leg, her dress was hiked up to her upper thigh, and it was difficult to keep my eyes off of it. So, I didn't try very hard. I stared intently at her thigh.

"Mr. Marmor," she screamed and opened her eyes wide unable to point at me with her broken fingers. "My eyes are up here."

"I know," I said. "Very astute." I had a towel wrapped tightly around my waist. It was soft as a plush toy and smelled new. I picked lint from it as I spoke.

"We all want to know one thing," Mr. Mills said, "why did you lock yourself in the bathroom for three days?"

"Excuse me? I took a bath, a bath that lasted no more than six minutes before it was so rudely interrupted by the appearance of that bubble monster thing," I repeated, "I was in there for only six minutes tops!"

Simon stolidly responded, "I hate to disagree with you, sir, but I must."

Mr. Mills began to berate me about lengthiness of my bath-time, but my thoughts drifted to the terror I had experienced during that bath-time. I could almost hear the bubbles popping, the monster cackling in my face, leaking its grime over me. After all, it felt as though I had only been in there for six minutes.

"You said that, sir. Twice," Simon said.

"Is he even paying attention?" Mr. Mills asked.

I thought I had only thought the thought. Turns out I had spoken said thought as I was thinking it and followed up with a description of each subsequent thought that I had thought. I tend to lose focus in deep conversations especially when boring people speak. These knuckleheads droned on and on about the amount of time I had wasted in the bathroom. I wanted to tell them that this conversation felt longer than my battle with the bubble-monster, but I didn't. I held my tongue.

"I'm glad you're taking this so seriously," Mr. Mills said sarcastically.

Without having to look at him, Simon said, "Yes, sir, you said that out loud."

"Do you want the good or the bad news?" I asked without waiting for an answer. "I'll give you the bad news first. Your house is haunted."

"And the good news?" Mr. Mills asked.

"Fortunately, you hired the best paranormal detective in the business." I puffed out my chest.

"Are you certain you weren't dreaming?" Mr. Mills asked pointedly, almost accusatorily as if I'd done something to earn his distrust.

"I am never certain of anything. I am only certain of what I saw from my own perspective. I never assume to presume that what I conclude I saw from my perception exists for the world at large. Who is to say that what they see is reality, and what they do not see is not reality? For I say that the world in which we reside is but a conglomeration of all the feelings and thoughts and sayings and emotions that we all share. So, I draw a line in the sand when you ask if I'm certain. To say that I can accurately tell you that the apparition I saw must exist for all would be laugh in the face of all philosophers before me. Ha! I would not be so bold. But, I can tell you that the ghost is German!"

"The hell are you talking about, bro?" Marc asked.

"I too am confused, sir," Simon said.

"German?" Mr. Mills asked.

"Now, however, in more pressing matters, this house is in fact haunted. I have looked the apparition in the eyes. I have stared death in the face. I have sniffed the taint of the afterlife. I have been chosen, the innocent, the sacrificial lamb, the only hope, the last Jedi. Maybe not the last one because that would be copyright infringement, I imagine, but I am sure I must fight this ghost to rid it from your house," I stated with such enthusiasm and vibrato that nobody dared to counter me. "I also now know its weakness. To expel this ghost from your humble abode, or not so humble, quite lavish abode if you ask me, we must find the heart. Enter the realm through a portal that only opens if we can summon the entryway to its lair. We must venture into the pits of Hell, find the apparition, and we must teach it etiquette!"

"What?!" all other parties in the room exclaimed except Simon who said, "What, sir?"

"The thing doesn't know manors. Obviously. Otherwise, it would not disturb such a restful peace I was enjoying during my bath time, and we must teach it not to bother, frustrate, irritate, antagonize, or generally annoy with its poor etiquette. If I can bring with me my commonplace etiquette book, which I carry with me at all times, I can do quick work of its bad habits, teach it appropriate propriety with which we all, even ghosts, ghosts particularly, should carry ourselves in a public setting, and cure you all of the pest's problematic behavior issues."

"We didn't bring you here to teach a ghost decency! We brought you here to get rid of it," Blanche said, like she might have stood if she were able to.

"Though not certain of anything, I'm fairly certain that I am the paranormal detective here. Not you, but I appreciate the insight, and I am open to constructive criticism," I assured not really meaning it.

"Get rid of it," Mr. Mills said.

"When I was but a youth, my mother told me, 'teach a man to fish, you'll need tartar sauce. Eat a man's fish, you'll be the tartar sauce.' And, I think that still applies."

"Definitely not how that saying goes," Marc said.

"You haven't met my mother. She says some pretty whacky things, and yes maybe my memory is bad, and yes, maybe I misquote her constantly, and yes, maybe eating fish and stealing fish are two completely different things, but gosh darn it, we're all people in this crazy, mixed-up world," I said, standing, "and instead of being divided by our words, why can't we all come together, work together, and teach this damn ghost some damn manners!" I raised both fists in the air triumphantly. "Are you with me?!" What a speech. What a good speech, I thought.

"Do you have to compliment yourself on your own speeches," Blanche said, irritated it seemed.

"Yep, sir. You said it out loud," Simon said.

"Yes," I said proudly, fists still in the air, breathing heavily to catch my breath, and then... WHOOSH!

A breeze blew through the room. The lights went out, and the room fell silent. Even Mr. Mills' computer charger's orange light shut off, possibly because, I'm guessing no electricity was running through the charger. Before I get into how ghastly the appearance of the ghost was, I just want to tell you about Mr. Mills' Macintosh laptop. It looked like a Mac Book Air, the thin, sleek metallic silver computer case looked pristine, most likely purchased within the last few months, gleaming almost as though he polished it daily. I have neither owned a laptop, nor have I been in an Apple store, but I have always dreamed of it. Yet, I find those geniuses to be frightening. When a customer does go to the genius bar, do geniuses serve knowledge the same way bartenders serve drinks? Apple is also prolific in its creativity. It continues to amaze me how often it releases new products, all with new attachments, and dongles, and whosits, and whatsits, and, not that I can afford it, but still, if you ask me Apple is killing the middle class. Where was I?

"The hell are you talking about Apple, dude?!" Marc said. "There's a ghost here."

"I'm thinking of getting a Macbook." I said.

"You don't know how to type, sir," Simon said.

"They do have dictation software! Don't they?! And don't mock me. I graduated top of my class from both high school and college."

"Because you were homeschooled," Marc said.

"Right again. Marc, you can be consistently right when you want to be."

"Will you idiots shut up and do your job! There is a ghost in my house!" Blanche shouted. "And, it's right in front of you idiots.

I finally gave the ghost my attention though my ego felt bruised from Blanche's insult.

From the rug beneath us rose a beast of beastly proportions. The carpet, like a geyser, towered before us, pulling us and all the furniture in the room towards the base of the being.

We all shuffled back, Mr. Mills falling out of his fancy chair as he dove for the floor, Blanche rolling backwards, Simon tucking and rolling almost ninja-like away from the thing, me crawling on my hands and knees like a baby on a treadmill, but Marc just stood there staring up at it with gaping mouth as if caught in its trance.

"No!!!" I shouted without saying the exclamation marks. Those are there for emphasis. Do not get confused, please. I watched as Marc got sucked in by the mountainous carpet that grew before us, an oriental, intricately patterned apparition.

And then it spoke, "Come here, *wenig* Marky. I just want to play a game. I want to play a game, little Marky, with your soul, little Marky. I want to drink your soul, Marky. I want your blood and your bones and brew myself a drink of your soul, and I'll drink it down. Drink it right down. MMMMmmmm. Marky. Don't you know how much I love my soul martinis. You'll be the *perfektes*, Marky Warky, you little snarky narky Marky." There standing before us was the monster with that same foul mouth. That same monster perforating his conversation with snippets of German, not that I know how to speak the damned language, but I could tell by the mucous it kept spitting up with each glottal stop.

Without speaking, jaw hanging slack, Marc inched towards the ghost. He was mute. Transfixed. His eyes looked like pale blank stars, bursting, imploding, his brain numbed by the ghost's bending finger. And, his feet stood planted to the carpet as he was pulled up the length of the carpet, completely parallel to the floor, his body completely paralyzed, his face heading straight towards the ceiling fan, which started to spin faster and faster and faster until it was almost spinning as fast as the blades of a helicopter, spinning so fast it looked it like it wasn't spinning at all.

As the carpet flew from under my knees, I felt the bare floor on my hands and felt that I had gotten a slight rug burn on the heel of my palm, and it irked me so. I hate rug burns. They linger, the pain, the sensation, boiling on the skin, annoying.

When I turned, I saw Marc's eyes inches away from the fan, his body completely straight. I shouted, "MARC! Don't listen to it!!!" again not saying aloud the exclamation marks. "Listen to me!" and I began to sing his favorite song. I sang it loud. I sang it with vigor. With vibrato. With perfect pitch. "Champagne, California on the brain. Got an appetite for no refrains. Just verses, she curses as blood vessels burst in defiance," and then Marc, snapping out of his trance sang along with me, "She made an alliance of the dark side of Hollywood!"

Suddenly, he was back, and he looked at me, "311. So good, man." One inch away from death.

"Limbo!" I shouted as Marc looked back up at the fan, spinning violently just in front of his nose. Marc was the champion of limbo nights at El Dorado, a small competition that he and I do one-on-one

74

with Simon holding a broomstick for us to limbo beneath. Marc won every single bout though I tended to cheat by tickling Simon and forcing him to raise the stick so I could get under it. And because he is my employee, I ask him to appease me, and he often does.

"Sir?" Simon said.

"Mmm. Oh yeah! LIMBO, MARC! LIMBO!" I said, and Marc leaned back. The fan spun wildly, violently, ripping into the air just before Marc's face as he bent farther back than I have ever seen a man bend. He bent until his back almost touched the carpet, and, though his head was now pointed directly towards the floor, he kept rising, as the carpet was being sucked into an abyss that the carpet was being sucked into.

Fortunately, though, Marc's face and body just snuck under the blades of the fan, and he cheered! "Win again, bitch!" Marc shouted at me.

I wanted to shout back that this wasn't a time for competition, but I knew that I could have won if I wanted to try. I just didn't want to try right then for fear of cutting of my nose. But, then my competitive nature took hold of me. I started to run after him.

"No, sir!" Simon shouted after me.

"I can't let that outrageous fool win!" I said angrily, almost knocking Simon back with my outstretched arm, like a running back making his way through a defensive lineman. Not that I know the first thing about sports. I ran to the fringe of the carpet, and I started my vertical climb up the vertical carpet wall, watching Marc's stupid face mocking me with sincere pride that he'd won a competition in which I'd never agreed to be involved in the first place!

But, his body was moving down, down, down as if into quicksand. Into the volcanic center of the carpet's newly formed black hole.

"I'll show you a winner," I said moving upwards towards the fan, which spun so fast I immediately regretted my decision to engage in the competition.

"I forfeit!" I said as I started to run backwards, backpedaling to stay as far away from the fan as possible. But Marc couldn't let it go.

"Undefeated, you little bitch! You're like ten inches shorter than me, and you still can't limbo for your life! Undefeated limbo champion right here. Marc Benjamin Reilly. In the house. That's this guy. Next round is on you, bitch! And you can go f—" but no longer could we hear Marc. He was sucked into the floor as he and the carpet vanished beneath the polished wood, now bare, as if through a hole, but when it was gone there was no hole left. Nothing to show where they'd vanished to. No sign of the monster. No sign of Marc. And unfortunately for me, I say with slight sarcasm due to the intense fear I felt as I was pulled towards it, the fan had stopped revolving so speedily and now just spun at a normal, kind of pleasant speed.

"Sir," Simon said, "I believe the wraith has taken Marc."

"You're probably right," I said spying the floor into which Marc had just disappeared.

"That was my best rug," Mr. Mills said.

"That was my best friend," I followed up. "I think it's about time we teach them both some manners. The ghost and that gloating oaf."

Blanche and Mr. Mills eyed me as if I said there were aliens living among us, which there are, no doubt. (I have had experiences with them, but those are stories for another time.)

I looked at Simon. "Now, boy! Here it is. Here is our primary concern from here-on-out. The ghost has our friend. It has taken him into his lair, and it's most likely doing ungodly things with him. And, by Jove, I think I know exactly where the key to finding him lies."

"Where, sir?" Simon asked.

"With him!" I pointed at Mr. Mills. "Did you note the ghost's accent and word choice?"

"No," Mr. Mills responded. Playing dumb. Obviously.

"The ghost is, and I know this because my grandmother was from there, a German Jew, a soul claiming vengeance on her life lost!" I shouted. "This means that the key to finding the spirit is in your Nazi collectible museum closet!"

"Nobody is allowed in there," Mr. Mills shouted looking at Blanche as if she would back her up, but instead she shrugged.

"I always thought your obsession with Nazi stuff was kind of weird," she said, pulling away from Mr. Mills.

"What? You can be obsessed with jewelry, but I can't be obsessed with a very critical turning point in world history?"

"Just saying. It's weird, Stephen," she responded.

"And so is your addiction to Selena Gomez's music."

"She's an inspiration to young women everywhere. You know what? Forget you," Blanche said and slowly, with great difficulty, wheeled herself from the room.

"If you want your rug back, I suggest you let me into your off-limits closet again because I'd also like to save my friend from certain death so I can beat him in a best-of-three limbo tournament, and because nobody in this room can make as good a Long Island as that man. So, let me look at your kampf, or we'll have to force ourselves in there anyhow!"

"Well put, sir. Very well put, sir," Simon said.

"Let the adults speak," I said to Simon. Sometimes he needs to be put in his place.

"Okay," Mr. Mills said, depressed watching Blanche finally make it out of the door and wheel herself squeakily down the hall. "Fine. It doesn't matter. Just do it."

"Wait. Really?"

Mr. Mills sat at his desk. "I just want to be alone," he said.

And I knew then that he just wanted to be alone. And, that Simon and I would be able to find this ghost, save the rug, rescue our friend, and fulfill our duty to our current contractors to protect them from this annoying apparition's aggravating antics.

Chapter 15

Simon and I set up in the living room, putting all of our gear back onto the floor and reassembling it, putting the broken pieces back together from our drunken playtime, getting ready for our descent into the madness in the lair of the being beneath the Mills' household. It was somehow, somewhere, alive within the house, deep in the construction's underbelly, a thing that could blend into the walls and floors, become the blender, be frozen with the ice in the ice tray, turn to porcelain and rise from the pipes. German engineering, this ghost.

After we laid our equipment before us, our outfits, our plasma-guns, our entrapping machines, our taxidermy ghost-sniffing cockroach Lucy, who we kept around more for morale than function, and the Ghost Mittens™ we stood like men ready to die. But I will be the first to tell you. I was not ready to die. I was ready to save a friend and teach a ghost the proper use of the terms *please* and *thank you*.

I inhaled slowly through my nose, held it for two seconds, and exhaled through my mouth when my heart stopped.

That's when I saw her. She was magnificent. A sultry goddess of perfect proportions. Smooth, buttery, caramel skin that honestly made me hungry. A tube top that clung to her rib cage like plastic wrap and displayed her stomach, which protruded slightly over the tight waist band of her denim skirt. Plump breasts that seemed to spill from her tight bra in all directions, a bra that hugged her so snugly that the extra skin of her upper body protruded from it and pressed against her white shirt so hungrily that it looked like it was eating any excess fabric. Her teeth were train-tracked with metallic pink braces that ran across both lines of her teeth, top and bottom, magnificently, as if they were meant for me and her to ride off into the sunset down them together.

I opened a Cliff bar and tore into it. I ate it so ferociously, I could feel the crumbs dribbling from my mouth onto the shag carpet beneath my feet. I wriggled my toes to try and cover up the debris that had fallen from my mouth, but it proved useless. I wound up just spreading the crumbs around.

She was an Indian woman of about twenty with hair like black ribbons and eyes like dark pools. This Indian goddess who seemed to materialize out of nothing looked at us with such disdain, I swear I could taste it, and it tasted terrible. Or, it was just the cardboard flavor of the peanut butter Cliff Bar, bits of which were still stuck in my teeth. She said, "The heck are you doing in my living room?"

I could barely form words. They were stuck in my Adams apple, or that too could also have been the Cliff Bar that I had ingested moments earlier, which was still making its way down my esophagus. Those snacks are extremely dry. They should be marked a fire hazard. Great joke. I'm a very good judge of comedic puns, and that one was a sure-fire ten.

I stared at her knowing that I had just fallen head over heels, dare I say, in love with her. For the first time in my life, I was in love.

"And who might you be?" I asked trying to maintain some element of composure, but I'm almost certain as I looked into Simon's eyes that the words barely came out of my mouth, and if they did they must've been majorly garbled because I look at Simon who looked at me with such confusion, it couldn't have been words, but being the good friend he is, he knew what I meant.

"This is Priya, sir," Simon said. "Mr. Mills' daughter."

"Adopted," Priya responded with a touch of attitude.

"You must be extremely fuel efficient," I said.

"I believe it's Priya, sir. Not Pryus, Simon said.

"And don't you screw it up again you smarmy a little furry little butt-munch," she snapped her gum in the most heart-achingly beautiful way I've ever seen.

"I see you've met my daughter," Mr. Mills said walking in, squeezing the bridge of his nose.

"Adopted, bitch," she said.

"Wonderful, isn't she," Mr. Mills said.

"I don't need you talking for me, *dad*. I can talk for my own damn self, so why don't y'all get to steppin' so I can get some sleep in this damn piece." Priya began to walk out of the room, but Mr. Mills stopped her with his hands on her shoulders.

"How was college today, sweetheart?" he asked.

She pinched his hands from her shoulders like dirty socks from a couch cushion and took them off of her. She walked by him, swaying as she walked out of the room with such grace that it made my head spin.

"You know how girls can be," Mr. Mills said.

"Beautiful," I said

"No need to be sarcastic," Mr. Mills said, "she's obviously quite the handful."

"What I would do to have my hands full of her," I said. "Of her butt," I clarified.

"I heard that," Priya shouted from upstairs, her voice ringing through the halls like a church bell. I could see it, our future, as the squealing sound of her high-pitched voice rang faded into the house, I saw our wedding day. A magnificent white dress with her stomach bursting with my seed, my growing child, the train of the dress trailing behind her curvaceous butt like a broken umbrella that one might find in a street garbage can after a heavy rain.

"I am her father, you know," Mr. Mills, grinding his teeth.

"Adopted," I reminded him.

"I feel as though I were reliving a scene from a Wes Andarson film," Blanche said as she rolled into the room. She rolled her wheelchair with her leg exposed, one gorgeous, leg exposed, sticking out towards me, casted and with a bare toe that stuck from its cast like a turtle head.

Mr. Mills tried to hold her, but she rolled right past him and towards me. She grazed my thigh and looked at me with her large, black eyes pleadingly. I could tell she wanted something. Maybe her lust for me was still percolating beneath her healthy bosom, despite my throwing her from the balcony. *Ehem.* I obviously mean, despite the ghost throwing her from the balcony.

But my mind was elsewhere. She spoke, but I could not listen. I was still thinking of my beauty, Pryus. Not the car but the girl. She was far more beautiful than a car, far more well-spoken, but far worse-smelling. You know that new car smell? She had the opposite. She smelled more like body odor, sweat, and fly paper.

I knew that Blanche was speaking to me because I could hear the airwaves vibrating against my eardrums, tingling with the sensation of sound, but I was neither paying attention nor caring to pay attention because my mind was upstairs, with my plump little Indian mistress.

Blanche kept droning on and on with the audacity that I could possibly be listening to her filth, the sound of her voice dwindling away to nothing but the irritating buzz of a fly.

"The hell is wrong with you?" asked Blanche, and she kicked me with her cast.

I looked to Simon to see if I had said what I had thought aloud. He nodded at me, the universal sign for *yes!* This told me that I had been speaking aloud about Blanche. I kicked her wheelchair back so she rolled back towards Mr. Mills, who caught her chair. I then made my way upstairs, to find the woman I so desired, Mr. Mills' adopted daughter, Pryus.

"Don't you dare go up there, you creep," Mr. Mills said, exasperated by the thought of having to chase me up the stairs, which he tried to do, but I was on the track and field team in my younger days. Though I was terrible during any meet, I knew I could beat Mr. Mills then. I knew it because I was running to my pleasure, to the object of my desire, to the woman who would bear my last name, and my firstborn, and my second born, and my third born, and potentially become the first woman that I ever divorced due to shifting visions of our collective future (maybe due to job placement, financial woes, infidelity, or even, and I don't want to discount it, considering the latest intercontinental news, nuclear war). Perhaps we would even die in each other's arms, depending on the longevity of our relationship. I am well aware, quite aware in fact, that 50% of marriages end in divorce, and I do not want to count us as one of the lasting for I did not want to jinx the love that I felt for her. Or at least the love that I thought I had for her. Or at least that feeling that I liked her a little bit and hoped that she might give me a little kiss on the cheek or something.

I knew I was on thin ice in my current position as ghost-hunter for Mr. Mills due to all of the difficulties I'd caused him. I knew that a lot was riding on this ghost-hunt, the money, getting back into the business, my pride. But, that feeling I got, that feeling I got when I saw the perfect beauty, that feeling when my heart skipped itself into a corner of my chest and started smashing itself against the cavernous walls of my chest. I knew I couldn't live without her.

I raced after his daughter with a thirst for something more than liquor, the elixir of the heart, the potion we call love. Still I was thirsty, I'd been thirty minutes without one of Marc's famous cocktails. How does a man survive without his bartender?

I ventured up the stairs and saw at the end of a long corridor the room of the girl I most admired in the world. There was a big sign on the door that read KEEP OUT, but I couldn't keep out. Love knows no barriers, no walls, no doors.

I entered her room, a man in love. A man with a heart ready for the embrace of a woman. A man with heart ready for penetration.

"My love," I shouted.

I couldn't bear to look into her brown eyes, but I knew that I couldn't survive any longer without her weight between my arms. I needed her more than I needed air, water, time, food, Jamba Juice, television, Fruity Pebbles, and alcohol (well, not alcohol. I mean, I'd definitely consider cutting down a bit. Maybe I could ease up on the morning drinking and the afternoon drinking and the night drinking. Well, no. I mean, definitely not cut down, but I could potentially drink each cocktail slower, but probably not. How about, let's just say, she could comment on my drinking on the rare occasion that I sleep-drink. But, not much. Actually, I really hate that, so maybe not. You know, thinking about it makes me thirsty. I could use actually a drink right now).

I couldn't look at her. What if she was in the midst of a conversation with another gentleman caller, maybe on FaceTime with him, or even, maybe, dare I say, Tinder! No! It couldn't be. It was too much to bear. So, I didn't wait to find out.

"Pryus, my love," I said. "Marry me!"

I fell to my knees, weeping at her feet. "Please. I can't be without you." As tears welled up in my eyes, I looked upwards, let my eyes run up her legs until I found her eyes, and then I saw it – her expression.

She was utterly terrified, horridly upset as if she, and I hate to use this expression ironically, had seen a ghost.

That's when it dawned on me. Slowly, my eyes tracked back down her smooth skin, and I found that she was completely, utterly, entirely naked. How I had missed it the first time confused me. Love must have skewed my detective abilities.

The curves of her body, bending and dripping over one another, creating more curves that made my stomach twist in knots with craving, but I could tell she was not of the same mindset as me, for she let out a shriek so shrill, it made me deaf in one ear for the following hour.

I took her scream as a cue that I was not wanted so I stood, bowed, and left the room to find Mr. Mills and Simon rushing towards the door.

"Not to worry," I said. "I believe there was a minor misunderstanding. Please excuse me while I wash the self-hatred from me with two liters of rum. Thank you very much."

I walked by their gawking faces down the hall and down the stairs, straight to the kitchen. I pulled two bottles of rum from the liquor cabinet, then walked to the living room and flopped down onto the couch. I took a pillow from the arm of the couch and screamed directly into the pillow with all my might, until my vocal chords almost gave out.

I took a drink.

Then screamed some more.

Chapter 16

"Look, not to cause an issue here, but I don't think I can keep you in this house," Mr. Mills said. "My daughter is deeply troubled, you having walked in on her nude, and yes, my tone is calm at the moment, but I do, really, very much, want to rip your head right off of your neck and shove it into the damn toilet. I swear on all that is holy you're lucky to only be fired right now."

"No," I said, as my attention turned to an oddity in the corner of the room. I walked away from the conversation and found myself nose-to-nose with a taxidermy German Shepherd. It looked so real I felt as though it could bark at any moment. Maybe it would bark if I just offered it the right kind of food. I had half of the Clyff Bar that I hadn't eaten from the moment I fell in love with the adopted daughter of Mr. Mills named after a hybrid, a quite popular hybrid, my sweet untouchable Pryus.

I pulled the bar from my pocket and thought to myself, *here, little doggy, here doggy!* This, I found out later from a private conversation with Simon that I had in fact said out loud, and did so for quite some time as I caressed the dog's stuff carcass in my arms.

"Don't touch Blondi!" Mr. Mills screamed.

"You're telling me that this is the creator of such hits as *Heart of Glass*, *One Way or Another*, and semi-hit *Call Me*. Yeah, I don't think so." The dog looked nothing like Debbie Hairy.

"Not the band. The dog," Mr. Mills said and took the dog from my hands. I then understood what women with postpartum depression must feel like.

"No, Dan. That's Blondi's dog. Hitler. No. Not that. That's Adolph Hitler's dog, Blondi."

"I'm confused. Adolph Hitler wasn't in Blondie."

"No. God. You have this way of weaseling into a man's mind with your nonsensical rhetoric. You are an idiot, and somehow you confuse me beyond belief, you annoying little..." Mr. Mills exhaled and did not finish his sentiment. "Adolph Hitler had a German Shepherd named Blondi, loved how obedient German Shepherds were. And this right here is a taxidermy replica of Blondi."

But, as he spoke, I thought of his beautiful daughter, adopted as she may be. The dog was fine and would make a nice mantel piece, but his daughter, I wondered, if she would be mine.

"She's beautiful," I said thinking of Priya and her wondrous rolls that dripped down her belly like curtains that are too long so that they bunch up against the floor.

"Isn't she? And loyal," Mr. Mills replied. "She even slept in his bed."

"I need her!" I said.

"Excuse me?" Mr. Mills asked. "That is a priceless artifact. She's not for sale."

"How dare you speak about your daughter like that!" I backhanded him across the face, "How dare you speak about her like that! For shame!"

"What the hell is wrong with you?" he said holding his face. "She can't hear us."

I was taken aback. "You mean, she's deaf." I looked upstairs and thought about my poor, dearest darling Priya unable to hear the beauty of her own voice, unable to indulge in my outpourings of sweet nothings, unable to listen to my vows, but alas, love is but a beacon we follow without discretion. "I don't mind! I would never listen to another song again if it would mean I could hold her in my arms for the rest of my life. Except for Semisonic's "Closing Time." I must always listen to that song before I retire to bed. And every song by Smashmouth. I love me some Smashmouth."

"It obviously can't hear anything. It's a dead dog."

I backhanded him again on the other cheek. "How dare you!" As Jesus says, make sure you turn both cheeks when a man mocks the woman you love.

"That is absolutely not what the Bible says, sir," Simon said.

I was appalled, and I cared not to question Simon if I had spoken aloud. I continued my tirade, warranted as it was. "That is a woman you're speaking about, and she's only a student! Give her a few years to find her way! Then you can mock her if she can't find financial stability!"

"What in God's name! What the hell are we talking about here?" Mr. Mills said with both hands on both cheeks.

"I believe Mr. Marmor is talking about your daughter, sir," Simon said. And, he was right.

Mr. Mills scoffed, but I could not be stopped. I was a man mad with love, and I would have shouted it from the rooftops if there was a safe ladder.

"I would do anything to make her an honest woman. You know what, sir? I would even play Blondie's discography on repeat if that makes her feel more at home. I would learn ASL. I would wear a red band around my arm, but not the Swastika because it's a little creepy and weird, no offense, but also awful. Actually, I probably wouldn't, if we're being honest here. I mean the Nazis were responsible for the deaths of millions of people, so it's kind of, you know, weird, but, I mean, also I understand your fascination with history, and I respect the freedom to intellectually pursue whatever it is you wish, as long as you're not harming other people, and not like killing dogs, and filling them with, I don't know, stuff, to make them look realistic, but I would never speak about my own flesh and blood, my own daughter, the way you just spoke about her. That Pryus is a good, reliable, ridable, trustworthy vehicle of my love, one that I would be sure to keep in good shape for the rest of her God-given life!" I said, exasperated as I found the end of my sentence. "What I'm really trying to say is… I need to save my friend."

Then, I slapped Mr. Mills as a punctuation mark. I slapped him three times just to be sure he knew I'd finished my soliloquy.

"Okay. Ow. Ow. Ow! Stop it!" Mr. Mills said as he pushed me away from him.

"What do you say? Please. Give me one more shot. I promise I won't let you down. Not you, Blanche, Blondi, Blondie, or Pryus."

"Fine. Then, do it NOW, and then get the hell out of my house." He got in my face. "And her name is PRIYA!"

"That's what I'm saying. Pryus," I said.

"Priya," Mr. Mills said.

"Exactly. Pryus," I said.

"PRI… YA," Mr. Mills said

"Pree-us," I repeated, in exactly his intonation.

"No, you imbecile. Priya," Mr. Mills said. Enraged now, but almost losing steam.

"Pryus. Yes. Exactly what I'm saying," I said knowing that I'd been saying it right all along.

"Okay. No. Say "prequel," like there should be a *prequel* of your life so we can see why you ended up such a dummy."

"Prequel."

"Now say "yum." As in, *yum* this meal is delicious."

"Yum."

"Now, without the M, say it again."

"Ya."

"Exactly! Put the two together, and you've got it! Pri-ya." Mr. Mills said as if he'd succeeded in helping me understand whatever it was he was trying to explain.

"Pryus," I said immediately. "I know. That's what I keep saying, and all you care about is eating and movie franchises. Not saying I don't care about both of those things, but you self-centered, inconsiderate, rude, crotchety, old man refuse to accept the fact that your daughter and I are destined to be together!"

And with that, Mr. Mills wound up, cocked a fist, and slammed his knuckles into my cheek.

It just so happens, right at that moment, I had become extremely sleepy and was in great need of a rest. The coincidence of the timing was remarkable. It might seem to the untrained eye that his punch knocked me out, that I lost consciousness because of the impact, but I assure you that is not the case. Right at that very moment, I made a very conscious choice to take a nap. It's odd, I understand considering that we were in the middle of a conversation, but I had been planning on falling asleep for some time. Yes, I fell to the floor. Yes, my body went limp. But, that is only because, and I assure you with a scout's honor though I was never a boy scout nor have I ever understood the tenants of the organization or what my saying scout's honor has to do with honesty. A scout can lie, too. I'm sure under the veil of constant veracity, that I was just putting my head down for a rest. I had grown weary with the pointless debate with my employer over his daughter's name, and it made my eyelids heavy, and my need for sleep great. So, right at that moment, I just closed them and rode with Queen Mab on her chestnut chariot into her world of dreams. It was by no means, and I don't know how to clarify this any further, the cuff of an old man that forced me into submission. It was pure exhaustion. I would never be ashamed to admit if the old man took me down in a fight, I promise. I would never be ashamed, and I would admit readily if a worthy foe had put me down for the count. But, in this very instance, it was definitely not him. I was just sleepy. Sleepy, I tell you. Don't press me any further regarding the matter because I will only tell you the same. It was a catnap, a power-rest, a snooze, a doze, some shut-eye, catching those z's. Nothing more. Nothing less. Got it?

When I awoke with Simon holding an ice-pack to my head as he is wont to do when I wake up in odd places, I knew then that I must stay and finish my duty, save this house from its surly ghost problem, rescue my friend from the depths of Hell, teach a ghost some proper manners, and then, only then, could I convince Mr. Mills that I was worthy of his daughter's attention, ask for her hand in marriage, and finally make my life whole with a celebratory Long Island Iced Tea.

Chapter 17

"Simon, am I an imbecile?" I asked. "I would say I'm more becile than imbecile. Wouldn't you agree, Simon?"

"It doesn't work that way, sir," Simon said.

I looked at myself in the mirror. I was ready. Geared up and armed for battle with the paranormal. I admired the black eye that was forming and thought, *do you think Pryus likes tough guys? If so, do you think I'm a tough guy? I wonder if Simon thinks I'm a tough guy.*

"Sir, I think all women like tough guys, but I would not call you a tough guy," Simon said.

"Who asked you?" I asked.

"You did, sir. Just now," Simon said.

I knew then that I had spoken out loud, but I wasn't embarrassed, as shown by the way I didn't care to correct myself.

"As I said, sir… Women like tough guys. You are not one," Simon said.

I did not like to hear that, and I think Simon could see the frown spread across my face because he instantly changed the subject, which brought my spirits up.

"I think we're ready, sir," Simon said.

"Locked and loaded," I said cocking my easy-cock, easy-aim, plasma pistol.

It was time. I knew before Simon had even insinuated that it might be time.

We walked down the long corridor, Simon and me, as if in slow motion. We looked cool, or in my imagination we did, and I will stick by that telling of the story even if we didn't look as cool as I hope we did.

We walked towards the door to Mr. Mills' memorabilia closet, but Blanche rolled after me. She said. "Be careful." She put her an arm in its cast out towards me, looked at me with her big eyes. "I think," she continued, "I think I love you."

I looked at her. Confused. What did she even mean? It didn't make sense. Had she lost her mind? Was she completely out of her gourd? Why would she love me? She must have had a screw loose, or a loose tooth because it sounded like she'd become completely and utterly baffled by the laws of society. She was just a nutter. A mad hatter. A basket-case.

"How dare you!" Blanche said, punching me in the groin and rolled away.

Doubled over, I looked to Simon for clarification, and he assuredly gave it to me. I had spoken loudly and clearly and all of my thoughts, even calling her a nutter, which is Simon's insult. Not just portions of my thoughts as I often do, but the entire paragraph of insults.

"She'll probably give us a bad Yelp review, huh," I said. "Remind me to write her a plea to give us a good Yelp review after we head back home."

"On it, sir," Simon said scribbling in his notebook.

The closer stood right before, obscured in shadows of the coming night. A bat hung from the top right corner of the door entryway. A spider web had been spun expertly on the top-corner of it. Thick strings of white web hung creepily.

"Those are Halloween decorations, sir," Simon said.

"No. Yeah. I know," I said straightening up and clearing my throat.

They were obviously plastic to the expectant eye. If I hadn't been so absolutely terrified of the festive ornaments, I would have obviously known they were fake.

"You sure you want to do this, sir?" Simon asked as he looked at me apologetically as if he could sense my fear.

I hadn't realized it until that moment, but I had jumped into Simon's arms, wrapped my hands around his neck like a smitten schoolgirl finding shelter in her beau's arms. Realizing my positioning, I pushed myself from his arms and landed on my feet.

"I obviously do. Where is Mr. Mills? Shouldn't he be here to warn us against going into his closet?" I said.

"He's upstairs consoling his daughter. She's a bit shaken, sir," he said.

"And Blanche? Where is she? Did you hear what she said to me? When she knows I'm already in a long-term relationship with Pryus."

"I'm right, here, asshole," she said from the other end of the hallway.

I turned the knob and walked through into the room armed and ready. "Let's do it," I said.

And we walked inside.

Surrounded by Nazi memorabilia once more, I felt off, like I was watching a Fox News report on repeat for hours on end, trying to understand how the network's agenda relates to the context of the world's actual events, or sitting in front of a babbling panel on some paranormal topic, totally distracted by the guy in the seat beside me is slurping on a juice box the entire time, trying to get the last drop out though we all know it's impossible. Sometimes the boxes will just have some juice left, and we all need to be okay with that. Sometimes, it's not worth it. The cost-benefit margin can't make the energy exertion worth the potential output. Especially if you're in a room of three hundred people, and everybody can hear you slurping for that last drop. We all know it's never coming! Why are you putting us through this? Let it go! How thirst quenching can that one drop be? Really. You drank the whole juice box. You don't need anymore. And, you're an adult. Don't have a juice box in the first place. That's like rule one. Drink out of a water bottle or even a soda can. Something that you must tip up to your lips. Something other than a juice box. Don't be a juice box guy. Ever. Really. Don't.

"Sir?" Simon said sipping from his juice box. He often suffered from low blood sugar, and he needed his boxes to recalibrate his system.

"Not you. In general. Did I say that out loud?" I asked.

"All of it, sir," Simon said.

"Great. Well, take it as a very important lesson."

"Will do, sir," Simon said dropping the juice box to the floor and stomping on it. He'd taken my rule to heart. Simon reached inside his backpack and produced a lollipop.

"And on that point, don't eat lollipops. They're for kids. Adults licking a lollipop is quite infantilizing. I can understand the need for a person fetishized but I don't agree with the consumption of lollipops on a daily basis," I said, leaning against a bronzed bust of Hitler that bent beneath my arm. I was about to proceed on the consequences of indulging in sugary snacks in general, but then the bent bust opened the archival, plush wall of Nazi pins like a revolving door. And I fell. Not Mein kampf-iest moment. Nazi puns: always a laugh holocaust.

Through the wall I went. Syntactic reversal. Otherwise known as poetic license, I fell down a winding staircase like a sideways slinky. Simile. Rhetorical devices. Imagery. Et cetera. I fell and I fell and I fell. It hurt and it hurt and it hurt. No matter what I did, nothing could stop the downward momentum of my body being hurled downwards, cascading down the stairs like I was being pulled by some invisible string, or more likely due to the invisible influence of gravity. My butt went straight over my head and crunched my back so much my crotch almost hit my face. I landed in a puddle of my own body, my sciatica acting up in a crescendo of pain as I attempted to prop myself onto my shoulder but couldn't.

Shortly thereafter, as I moaned like one of the ghosts we were supposed to be hunting, Simon walked down the stairs calmly. "Are you okay, sir?" Simon asked acknowledging my pained face with a sympathy that might be comparable to a goldfish watching a murder. No real sense of understanding of the severity of the situation.

"Help me up, you buffoon!" I shouted.

I held my hand out.

"I don't take kindly to that sort of name calling. Just because you feel bad that somebody called you names doesn't mean you need to demean me," Simon said. "Two wrongs do not make one right, sir." He left me to flail on my rump, reaching for him wildly. I felt like an old tortoise that had rolled onto its shell.

"My mother used to tell me that," I said. "She used to say, two elbows to the gut don't make a steak salad taste any better."

"She was right," Simon said back. "But I don't see the correlation."

"The mouth on you!" I said attempting and again failing to stand on my own accord. "That's my mother you're talking about!" I put out my hand again, but Simon just crossed his arms awaiting my apology.

"Simon," I said. "I'm sorry." I know Simon. I saw his lip curl slightly at the thought that I may have apologized to him for the first time in my life. Then I hit him with the rest of the sentence, "...that you think I'd apologize to you for anything because I have nothing to apologize for." This time, I stood by myself. Easily. Ok, not easily. With some definite struggle. But, I managed to stand. To hammer my mockery home, I quipped, "What's your IQ? Like 50."

Simon didn't retort, but I know his mother used to tell him his IQ at the end of every phone call, and I would always razz him about it.

She'd call him the Dolph Lungren of the U.K. His IQ was and most likely still is north of 160, and his mother always called him a special boy, loved by his family, all of whom were waiting for his safe return to the land of his birth. He was all too humble to say anything regarding how much of a genius he was, but I knew it because I had tapped his phone at an early moment in our friendship and listened to every outgoing call he ever made.

"Why are you so mean? You know you're wrong, and you still mock me, sir?" Simon screamed. And then, having lost his temper for the first time I'd ever seen, Simon looked almost embarrassed.

"Wrong?! Ha! My behind," I said brushing past him, completely aware that I was making a big deal of something so that I wouldn't have to think about the humiliation I had just endured. I was over-compensating. Feeling both inept for falling down the stairs and being unable to get back up, I needed to retaliate against somebody who to reaffirm my power as a human. Thus, I took things out on Simon. I felt bad about it, sure, but I'd never admit it. Not to Simon. Not to anybody. These are the dark secrets I like to keep buried deep within me, things I never can tell anybody. My feelings of self-loathing and self-deprecation. Those feelings and thoughts must be shunned, exiled from the mind, sequestered into the deepest parts of the psyche, the parts of the psyche that, without use, wither into nothingness, repressed like hated step-children. I have learned that these thoughts might potentially boil up from the emotional basement and erupt from my mouth at unexpected times. Like being cut off in traffic, or not getting the enough popcorn at the movies when sharing a bag with a friend, or during long walks alone. Sometimes, those are the times these horrid feelings come out. But, I'd rather these outbursts occur than deal with my emotional incompetence.

"Very self-aware. And poetic, sir," Simon said.

"Huh?" I said. "Shut up, dweeb, and let's keep moving!" I shouted.

Simon shrugged to nobody as if to say, *best I can do.* And we walked down a long corridor, bricked stone arching over us, as the tunnel floor extender at a six-degree descending slop. Luckily, I had my crank flashlight so I could light the way, and I cranked and cranked as we made our way farther and farther beneath the house, into the belly of Silver Lake, the depths of Los Angeles.

Then I farted. Just for fun.

Chapter 18

The basement was the epitome of creepy. It reminded me of the time when I wasn't even ten years old and I first ventured into Mrs. Norman's house in the Palisades. I remember it well. She'd gone for a vacation somewhere in the mountains, and she left the door wide open. As a youth, I walked inside just to see what old people lived like. I'd always been curious. The smell of moth balls and lint and oldness. It almost poured from her door onto the street where I rode my bike. There'd been rumors she murdered her husband and hid his body in the freezer. That was the moment my ghost-hunting fantasies became something tangible. Because I felt it. Right when I walked inside. The cool chill when his spirit passed. The heavy pressure on my chest. I remember it well. I was so terrified that I fainted.

Then it turned out I had fainted from carbon monoxide poisoning. That's why she had left for the mountains. People were coming to check out the leak the next day, and there I went into the heart of the gaseous leak. When I came to in the hospital, I asked my dad if ghosts actually existed. He looked at me like it was time he had to have the talk with me. Hunting ghosts was like sex to him. He loved it. It made him so elated, he looked relieved to finally unburden himself of the secrets of his occupation. I could see it in his eyes after he explained it to me, that it was euphoria to him.

The next week, I started as his apprentice. And it's been one day after the next in my new passion as a ghost-hunter.

Now, that same fear was building up within me again. Pressure. Chills. Fear. But, now I knew it wasn't carbon monoxide poisoning. After many a mishap, I'd finally learned the difference.

As we made our way deeper and deeper into the musty basement, my nose began to burn. The place smelled like bitter almonds, or moldy peach pits. It was a scent I couldn't place, but it made me hungry. My eyes began to water. My throat started to itch.

"Do you have my epinephrine?" I asked Simon quickly, coughing as I choked on my own saliva.

"You don't have allergies," Simon said, "except to Amoxicillin. As you persistently remind me, sir."

"Of course. Then why do I feel as if I'm having an allergic reaction to amoxicillin?"

"I sense it, too, sir," Simon said.

Simon bent down to one knee and reached into his satchel that he always carried at the ready. The sound of him unzipping the bag reverberated off of the walls throughout the corridor, echoing down the hallway. From his bag, he pulled a foldable set of equipment: his Air Quality Measurement Kit, as he declared while unfolding it. He liked to narrate for me exactly what he was doing at all times, especially when it pertained to his equipment, as if that would convince he knew what he was doing, but I never paid attention. Still don't. Honestly, as I write this, he's talking about some nonsense global warming contraption he designed to cool the atmosphere that could potentially save millions, blah, blah, blah. Don't care.

Nonetheless, as asked, Simon has provided me with a transcription of exactly what he said to me that day. He always records our conversations on his cell phone for prosperity, or in case of any workplace abuse, sexual harassment, or anything else of the sort. I don't mind because when he sleeps I usually delete any of the day's conversations that paint me in a bad light. I know his phone's password and his mom's maiden name. Anyhow, here's the transcript of Simon's lengthy discussion about his contraption for testing the air quality:

"Here," Simon said, "I've taken a TSI Alnoore ABT511 Balometer capture hood." At this moment, he unfolded a dark blue cone connected to a small rectangular meter beneath. "I then connected it to a Model PHT 18000 Hardness Tester modified with a Phase II Rockwall Metals Detector, supplemented by a dehumidifier to pull all the air into the chamber to test for all pollutants containing any element on the periodic table. Any toxic chemical created from 1910 up to today should show up when I turn this bad boy on, sir," Simon said.

He connected the blue cone to a small meter, uncoiled a wire to a machine that had buttons and numbers and LEDs flashing on it. He pressed a button, and his contraption stated to whir almost uncontrollably. The machine began to tremble beneath the surge of the electrical input and air intake.

Fifteen seconds passed of inscrutable and chaotic loudness, which could have left a small child deaf in one ear. Fortunately, I had Simon. I knew for certain that he kept earplugs in his pocket at all times. He asserts that this is because I snore, though I have assured him I do not. I've never heard it, and he has no proof, so without irrefutable proof that I snore, I can rightfully say that I never snore. I also make sure to delete all video evidence from his phone of me sleeping to make sure he could never demonstrate the opposite.

Anyway. When he reached for his earplugs to put them in his ear cavities, I nabbed them and shoved them deep into my own. I could feel my excessive ear wax compress in my ear, and I blamed Simon for it.

As I plugged my ears, Simon cupped his hands over his own, holding the mechanism in his armpit. So he didn't need the earplugs anyway. QED.

I began to sneeze uncontrollably as the air was stirred, and it felt as if my allergies were worsening. I could feel the snot dripping from my nose into my mouth. It tasted like blood. I wiped the snot away and realized that it was, in fact, blood. I was bleeding from my right nostril. So was Simon. I couldn't believe it. Every time I see I'm bleeding, it reminds me I'm human. Though other animals bleed, too, at least mammals and maybe also fish and reptiles. Birds? So maybe I'll come back to this line of thinking later.

In any event, just as the sound had begun, it stopped.

Simon looked at his measurement system, and he gave a resounding gasp. "Zyklon B!" he shouted.

I pulled out my ear plugs and handed them to Simon. "What?" I asked as he eyed the wax-caked tips of the plugs with genuine disgust.

"Zyklon B," he said again as he dropped the plugs to the floor. "It's the chemical used during the Holocaust in the gas chambers at Auschwitz. It often gives off the smell of bitter almonds and was once used as a pesticide in America before it was banned."

His explanation lasted much longer than necessary, and I again found myself tuning him out. From the sewer system beneath and the cracks in the stone walls, a vapor filled the room. The smell got stronger, more intense.

"Nazis. I despise Nazis," I said, not usually one to have strong emotions. But I felt at that time that they deserved it.

"Zyklon B is known for killing those who inhale it in twenty minutes or less, sir," Simon said pulling a gas mask from his satchel and strapping it over his head.

"Hand me mine, Simon!" I shouted, covering my mouth with my shirt.

"You told me you didn't need it, sir," Simon said.

"I never said such a thing," I said.

He already has his phone cued to a particular voice recording of mine, and he let it play, "I don't need my gas mask. When the hell have I ever needed my gas mask?!"

"I always keep backups of recordings, sir," Simon said. "That was you circa 2012, sir."

"That could have been anybody," I said! "How do you know it's me?"

Then he played the next part of the speech, "I'm Dan Marmor! I assure you on my life that I'll never ever, and I repeat, ever need a stupid gas mask."

"Check and mate," I said.

He put his phone away. And I began to get woozy. I felt my feet reeling beneath the weight of my body, spinning beneath me, as I coughed and coughed.

"Zyklon B can make you dizzy, can cause hallucinations, and it can eventually make a man lose his mind completely, sir," Simon said.

"That's okay, because I feel completely fine," I shouted, completely not fine as more vapors filled the hallway. It felt like we were walking deeper and deeper into a haze, like we were encompassed by a cloud, but a bad cloud, one that could tear about your lungs.

And at that moment, a vision appeared before us as more gas poured in around us. It laughed, the vision, the apparition, the fearful ghoul.

It was a ten-foot tall ghost, with a gaunt face, thin bird-like lips, huge ears, beady little eyes, slicked back, black hair. A green, double breasted jacket, a green tie, and a bright red armband around his left arm, with an insignia on it. A swastika, made of snakes, all hissing, all writhing, alive within the white circle that hooped around them. His hands were clasped in front of him as his long, split tongue shot out of his mouth as he cackled, "BWAHAHAHAHA!" His laughter even rang out with a German accent.

"Who are you?" I shouted! "Where is my friend? Where is Marc?"

"Your Irish insolent bosom buddy is indisposed at the moment." The ghost cleared his transparent throat, "I am Dr. Goebbels," the ghostly villain cackled. "And, these are my children!" Goebbels said in a thick German accent, and he raised his hands, palms upwards.

Five pale wisps of ghost-children rose from the ground, four young girls and one young boy, all blonde, all with dead-blackened eyes, breathing the gas from their smoking mouths, flicking their forked tongues. They hissed with great relish.

I choked on the gas as the ghost of Goebbels stared at me with contempt, and his children hissed at me, snapping like Cobras, ready to gouge me with their fangs, poised for attack.

"Give me Marc before I destroy you and these kids!" I said through gasps. I could feel the time ticking away as my body felt weak and my mind even weaker.

"Puny human Jewboy! I do not listen to those still on the mortal coil, especially those as insignificant and poor as you. What do you think you can do? Ya? I am the Doctor of all Diabolic! The Lieutenant of the Luftwaffe. The—"

"Dude! I really don't care," I said. "You are super boring. Let's just fight, you Ghost Nazi."

I raised my fists as the ghost looked at me, mouth agape. Like he was used to finishing his speech as those he taunted and intimidated allowed him the time to finish his ridiculous monologue.

"Okay," the ghost of Goebbels said, "Go, mein Kinder. Kill the infidel Jew!"

Goebbels' children approached, hissing, weaving like snakes through the smoke.

Feeling off-kilter, seeing double, I called for help. "Simon! I said, "Hand me the Ghost Catcher 3000!" I held out my hand to take my ghost-gun, but Simon refused to hand it to me. "If you're mad at me, let's talk about it later. Just hand me the damn Ghost Catcher 3000!"

The children kept approaching, and Simon still hadn't handed me the piece of equipment, the only piece that might help us in this situation.

When I looked back to Simon, I saw him lying on the floor. Down and out. Then it hit me. Marc and I had tampered with his mask a long time back. We had modified it into a smoking contraption, one that most might refer to as a vaporizer, not that I smoked marijuana often, but I had seen it online and wondered if Marc and I could transform the gasmask into something that also burned the newly legal substance. And it had worked. He had turned what once was an electric gasmask to turn it into a marijuana vaporizer, so that when the user turned it on, it would create huge inhales of the substance called hash, the resin of condensed marijuana, burned at a very high temperature, and with three deep breaths, that modified gasmask could probably get an elephant stoned.

"Whoops," I said, as the snapping ghost-children approached.

And it hit me… "Wait. Wait. Wait. Are these like Jewish kids from the camps? Or are these your kids? Like Nazi kids?"

"These," Goebbels hissed, "are of mein own flesh and blood, Harald, Halga, Helmut, Holdine, Hedwig, and Heidrun. I brought them into this world and trained them to murder the Jew. They thirst for Jew-blood. They are the sworn enemy of the Jew, and it looks like you whet their appetite!"

Goebbels' children continued to approach with fingernails like blades and eyes like black holes.

"So, like, ethically speaking, purely hypothetically speaking, I can like kill them and not feel totally bad about it? I mean, I'm completely against killing kids, especially ones that met worse deaths than I can fathom, but like… on grounds of self-defense, and that they're, like, your kids and the undead, does that make it kind of okay?"

Simon woke momentarily, a moment, "It's fine, sir. Just kill them!" He coughed and fainted again.

I knew then what I had to do. I took up the air-testing meter in my arms and held it before me like a weapon.

"Come at me, Ghost Nazi-bitches!" I said, and I flipped the switch. It kicked into gear like an F1 racer roaring into fifth gear. VRRRRRR! It sounded through the corridor. I could feel its power in my hands as it vibrated ferociously. The Nazi Ghost children stared at one another, confused as to what was happening, but slowly I could see particles of their faces vanishing into the Air Quality Tester.

Lo and behold, it worked! The children began to whimper, "Papa! Papa! Hilfe!" They were instantly sucked into the machine, the girls first and then finally the boy, all hissing with great intensity as they were pulled into the machine.

"Mein kinder!" Goebbels wailed as his children vanished into the machine. I used Google Translate much later to learn what all of these German words meant. I mean, I didn't, but I had Simon do it for me. And then I forgot them. I include the sounds I remember here so that you can look them up. If you're that kind of person. That is, if you're a nerd.

Back to the action.

As the last boy's face vanished into the machine, I turned my attention on Goebbels' ghost. His gaunt face and his engorged belly all made me queasy. That, or it could have been the Zyklon B.

"You're next!" I said, holding the machine out towards him aggressively. At that moment, I got the chills. I felt like Stone Cold Steve Austin, my childhood hero. I only wished I had a metal chair so I could wield it above my head like a sledgehammer and slam it down with biblical fury; I also wished I had a twenty-four pack of Cooers Light so I could get sufficiently wasted while reading from John 3:16. I saw his face start to pull from his ghostly spirit as I pulled him into the air tester.

He was almost completely sucked into the machine, and I was beginning to feel a sense of triumph, ease, excitement to rid the basement of this ghastly villain. That's when the meter clogged. Without ceremony. Without warning. Much like pulling the plug from an outlet when you push the vacuum just a little too far from the wall. With his balding forehead sticking out from the air tester, I smacked the machine, trying to get it to work again, but it merely sputtered and died. Goebbels stared at me with expectant eyes, like he was ready to vanish from existence but hadn't completed his journey. I shrugged. "I promise that never happens," I said. "It usually lasts longer. I swear."

Goebbels laughed! "You impudent Hebrew! Doesn't matter anyhow. I killed those kids once. Watching them die again, I couldn't care less."

"You're a monster," I said.

"True," Goebbels' ghost bellowed with laughter as his fingers turned into snakes, and unfurled towards me. Their teeth dripped with venom. Their tongues, shooting and darting with gaseous vapors, approached me.

"Damn it, Simon!" I said throwing the machine into Simon's stomach, which woke him from his peaceful rest. He sat up quickly and pulled the mask from his face, giggling.

"What happened, sir?" he laughed.

"Oh, nothing," I said, "we're just going to die at the hands of this ghostly Nazi! Just another Wednesday. You know." If he didn't pick up on the thinly veiled sarcasm, I'd say he was denser than he thought me.

"I don't see him, sir," Simon said, his eyes bloodshot, and his vowels slow and extended, giggling the whole time.

"Who are you speaking to, you dirty Jew-man!" Goebbels said as he floated towards me.

I could feel the Nazi ghost-snakes getting ever so near, the warmth of their scaly skin so close, their sharp teeth just inches from my face. Goebbels' ghost laughed even louder than Simon as it got closer.

"You don't see him?" I asked Goebbels.

"Who?" Goebbels said angrily. "Don't waste my time, and die like the others before you. Purge the world of your disgusting dreidels." I knew then based on what Goebbels had just said that he couldn't see Simon.

"And you don't see the ghost?" I asked Simon.

"I'd help you, sir, but I don't see what you're talking about!" Simon giggled. "I must be too high, sir," Simon said.

"That's it!" I said. "The vapors of THC cancel out the vapors of Zyklon B!"

"Sorry. That makes no sense, sir," Simon said. But it was too late, I ripped the gas mask from his fingers, and I put it on.

"That's mine!" Simon said giggling. "I was using it, sir."

I stood there, still as the snakes flicked their tongues at me, dripped their venom on my cheek, and hissed in my ears.

"What time is it, Goebbels?" I said with a smile.

He looked at his wrist. He flicked it with his tongue. "My watch is dead. Must be a ghost watch," Goebbels said.

"No," I said. "It's four twenty, you Nazi scum." I put the gasmask on, pressed the button, and took a huge inhale. Now, I remind you, I never indulge in marijuana. I never partake of the devil's herb. I merely like the smell. But, this was business. I inhaled as deep as I could, puffed out my cheeks as the vapors of the weed filled me.

I ran towards him, weaving in and out of his snaking fingers, making sure not to get bit by the gaseous serpents. Maneuvering like a running back towards Goebbels, I managed to duck and weave through his snapping tendrils, and I jumped towards him. In high school, I was known for my vertical. Despite being below average height, I could almost touch the rim when I played basketball. Any time we had a pickup basketball game, I was chosen second to last, which made me feel quite good about myself. I was no Randy Sturdevant. That moron could barely dribble. Okay, I couldn't touch rim, but I could definitely net. Okay, I couldn't touch net. But, I could jump over a garbage can without clipping it. Okay, I'd clip it a little bit, but only a little bit. But, still. We can all agree that Randy Sturdevant was worse than I was. Okay, he was a bit better. Okay. He was a lot better. I never even played. This was all a hoax. I'm pretty bad at jumping, but this time, with all the adrenaline pumping, I guess I found that I could jump pretty high.

Right then, I jumped so high, almost six feet, so high that I could reach the ghost's face.

I jumped and I took off the mask, jumping so that my face was right in front of his face. And, I exhaled shot-gunning the marijuana smoke into his mouth.

"Vape his ass, sir!" Simon shouted as I flew through the air in what felt like slow motion.

And, Goebbels, mid-laugh, inhaled. Stopped. Through the vapors, I could see Goebbels' eyes instantly turn bloodshot, his laugh higher pitched with every burst of air from his diaphragm. And as he laughed, I started to faint. I could feel my life escaping from me, pulling into the atmosphere, the Zyklon B wreaking havoc on my internal organs. I could feel that it was almost my time. Or I was just extremely high. I can never tell the difference.

"Simon," I said, almost with my last breath, "don't touch any of my stuff… And, feed… my cat!"

"You don't have a cat, sir,"

"I know… Buy a cat… Then… feed it. In my memory," I said, and collapsed. I could feel my last breaths coming.

And, then Goebbels' ghost began to giggle so loudly, the room shook. His eyes turned so red, he looked like he'd been possessed by the Cool-Aid Man. He sounded like a murderous, flaming chipmunk.

His spirit began to twirl and bound through the space, as his gaseous, corporeal slammed from wall to wall. As the being ping-ponged through the corridor, it began to dissipate. It began to unravel. The snakes began to wilt like dead roses. Goebbels' face began to melt like a Dali painting. His clothes began to decay like rotting fruit.

And as he had appeared, he vanished. As did the Zyklon B.

Simon ran to me, "SIR!" he cried. "Mr. Marmor!" he said. "DAN!" he shouted, and knelt down crying by my side. The tears formed in his eyes and dripped onto my face.

That's when I burst into laughter. I open my eyes and laughed so hard my abs hurt. It hit me then that I hadn't done crunches in a long time.

"You're alive," Simon said bewildered.

"You should have seen your dumb face, crying!" I laughed.

Simon stood and brushed his eyes. "I was just impressed you managed to defeat the ghost, sir" he said. "I was crying out of admiration."

"Yeah, right!" I bellowed in his face.

"How did you do it, sir?" he asked wiping the tears from his eyes.

"It's obvious, my dear Simon," I said holding out my hand for him to help me up. "When I realized that you couldn't see Goebbels through your intoxicated eyes, I knew that the vaporizer was the thing that would begone the ghost."

"That's not a word, sir," Simon said.

"So when I pushed the vaporizer button on the gasmask and inhaled, breathing that smoke into the mouth of the ghost himself, I knew that the two chemicals compounds would eliminate one another."

"Fortunately, I was right," I said, "Or I'd be dead. Turns out marijuana saved my life!"

"It is a medical substance, sir," he said. He took my hand and helped me up.

"Right," I winked. "You stoner dog, you."

"I don't smoke, sir. You know that. You tampered with my gas mask!" Simon shouted.

"You say tomato, I say tomato," I said.

"You have no idea what that saying means. It doesn't have anything to do with this scenario, sir," Simon said. "And, you said tomato the same way twice, which completely undermines the associated sentiment of the platitude."

"Come on," I said. "We have a friend to save!" I pointed to Simon's satchel. He picked it up. "Oh, and by the way. Your machine thing is broken," I said.

Simon picked it up and it fell apart in his hand, broke into pieces and fell to the floor. "That cost three thousand dollars, sir," Simon said.

"Put it on my tab," I said, as we continued deeper into the basement. Then I looked back at him and delivered my punchline. "Not!" I said.

Chapter 19

We continued deeper into the stone archway as it got danker and danker, mustier and mustier, ghostlier and ghostlier. It now smelled sweet, like moldy, stagnant water. I handed the crank flashlight to Simon so he could light our way farther.

The crank spun with a soft and slow ERRRAAHH, ERRRAH, ERRRRAH, squeaking as it turned due to a rusted gear from when I left it outside during a Christmas vacation during which I participated in an igloo building contest. I came in last, due to the structure caving in on me within the first twenty minutes of building time. I had quit then, when I was behind. I mean, isn't that what you're supposed to do —

ERRRAHH! ERRRRAHHHH! The noise continued nonstop as Simon continued to turn the crank. It grated on the eardrums. Not only that, but Simon couldn't help himself from humming along with it. Why must the pour oaf constantly hum?!

"It's not me, sir" Simon said, interrupting my thoughts.

"Why must you always do that? Interrupt my thinking like that," I chastised. "It's rude."

"You were speaking aloud, sir," Simon said. "You said my name at least six times!"

"Quiet," I shouted, raising one finger in the air to stop him from speaking. The sound of humming continued, and I knew that Simon could not speak and hum simultaneously. The voicebox doesn't work that way. Unless Simon could possibly create such a dichotomy with his voice, then he'd be a ventriloquist extraordinaire. But, I was certain at the time that he couldn't possibly hum and speak at the same time. However, now that I write this, I 'm unsure whether or not I should have been so certain before because Simon is the kind of person who would take the time to master such an inane talent.

"I can't hum and speak, sir," Simon said.

"Why do you always interrupt me while I'm thinking, Simon?!"

"Because," Simon shouted. "Look!"

"At what?" I said staring at him.

"At that!" Simon shouted pointing straight ahead. I followed his outstretched finger and found where he was pointing. That's where I saw it. It was a rotund, round-headed ghoul with round glasses, shaved sides of the head and a small patch of blonde hair on top. He looked like Tin-Tin but also not. He looked like a huge nerd, a real big dweeb, if you ask me. The swastika around his arm and the iron cross on his lapel made him look even dumber. I'll be the first to say it. Nazis are super lame.

"Where's our friend?" I shouted into thin air. "Where's Marc?" But it was almost as if the ghost heard me but continued to ignore me. And, boy, do I hate being ignored. It makes me feel invisible. Like a ghost. Maybe, that's why I hate ghosts and hunt them for a living. Maybe that's why ghosts hate people and haunt them for a living.

See what I did there?

The ghost hummed a song; I couldn't place it. I hadn't ever heard it before. It had a nice lilt to it.

"Lili Marlene, Simon said, "a famous song during World War II for both German and British forces. This particular version was sung by Marlene Dietrich. Himmler had a special liking for this song." Simon was such a know-it-all.

"Lili Marlene, I knew it!" I said to Simon. "You didn't have to tell me!" The big Nazi ghost continued approaching, still humming. And, I knew I then as he hummed. This was Heinrich Himmler, the head of the SS. I knew that because Simon told me, but I refuse to give him credit for this particular knowledge.

"Alright, Humming Himmler," I said. "What do you want? We got places to be. People to saves. Ghosts to train."

Himmler began to sing,

> *"Give me a rose to show how much you care.*
> *Tie to the stem a lock of golden hair.*
> *Surely tomorrow, you'll feel blue.*
> *But, then will come a love that's new."*

"Simon. Did I bring my trusty rose?" I asked.

"You don't have a trusty rose, sir," Simon said.

"I did at one point. Or, maybe I bought a rose from the store once. Or, I saw a rose somewhere once. Or, I saw the word rose once before. But, now that you mention it, it does seem like an odd request." I turned my attention to the ghost. "That's an odd request! Why do you want to me to give you a rose?"

Himmler continued to approach, still humming, still singing. He snapped now as he sang, as he approached. Lightning formed at his fingertips. Each snap lit the room with a sudden flame of electricity. He dragged his back leg with him as he walked. It scraped along the basement floor, sending off sparks.

I cracked my neck. "Alright, Heinrich. If that's how you want to play it." I raised my fists. I had grown up a boxer. Okay. Not really. In Kindergarten, my teacher, Mrs. Ludlow, held a baby fight club, and though I never won a fight, I did get the Sparkplug award. Had a lot of heart. Despite my 0-52 record, I approached the Nazi wraith.

I wound up, reeled back, my fist preparing for the glorious connection of knuckle on flesh, but as I did, Himmler snapped and vanished.

"Come back here and fight like a man," I shouted to nothing. "Or what once was a man!"

The whistling of Lili Marlene filled the space, coming from here, then there. Then up. Then down. And the room began to shake violently.

The walls began to close in on us.

"Quick. EVP. Stat!" I shouted to Simon.

"What's the magic word, sir?"

I said, "I said. Quick. Electronic Voice Phenomenon Detection machine. Now. And when I say now, I mean now. Before we die an unnatural death."

"Sir, no offense, but your tone has been quite curt recently, and it's starting to hurt my feelings. So, you'll not be getting your EVP until you either say the magic word or apologize, sir," Simon said.

"Now you decide to put your foot down?" I asked as the walls closed in around us.

"A man can only take so much, sir," Simon said, wiping a tear from his eye.

"I am not sorry. I have nothing to be sorry for." The walls kept caving in around us.

"Then good luck finding the ghost of humming Himmler, sir," Simon said with spite, crossing his arms over his chest like a child in the throes of a temper-tantrum.

"Let me get this straight. You'd prefer to die than hand over a piece of equipment because I don't say the word *please*?"

"In short: yes. In long: yes, you savage," Simon said. "You know the real evil we've been looking for. It's been right here all along. It's you, sir!"

I gasped, taken aback. "How dare you!" I said. The whistling grew louder, and the ghost swam beneath my legs, knocked me from my feet. I landed on my back. Again. My back being the most sensitive part of my body. "Give it!"

"No!" Simon said.

"Simon. Now!" I shouted.

"Not until you say the magic word!"

I looked at Simon. I could feel the cold breath of the ghost on my face. It was breathing in my life force, each inhale leading to a tirade of whistles.

"Please…" I said.

"That's all you had to say, sir," Simon said handing the EVP to me. I took it from him and smiled.

"…don't be so nebbishy!" I could see the hurt in Simon's face, which made the burn that much more satisfying. "Check and mate!"

I fired up the EVP, remodeled to not only detect supernatural sounds, but also to emit a negative frequency, thus cancelling out the noisy ghost. Like noise-cancelling headphones, except for the physical matter of apparitions.

The walls had nearly closed around us as the EVP loaded, its screen taking its sweet time. The battery-powered device often struggles to load fully. Finally, when the detection signal reached full, I pointed it straight ahead — only to find that Himmler was straddling me, his ghost member in his ghost hand right over my face. I was being dyslexic-Wienstien'd!

"Oh my God. What the hell are you doing, you fiend?" I shouted

Humming Himmler looked down at me, caught red-handed. His eyes wide, he stopped moving.

"You dirty devil," I said as I slammed down on the EVP activation button. It calibrated to the sound of Himmler, his ectoplasmic vibration, signaled him out, and it produced a noise undetectable to the human ear but which resonates in the human stomach. Like the bass from a subwoofer in your friend's car that he makes you sit listen to even though you're not going anywhere, it whips through your chest and gives you tinnitus for three days afterward.

The EVP released its decibel-imprisonment-system just in time, just before Himmler released his ectoplasmic revenge all over me. The walls stopped shuddering. The ghost-Himmler stopped humming. And the whole room settled. The wall's stopped closing in on us, and Himmler stopped whistling, stopped being, vanished. Even worse, he'd been vanquished. Dan Marmor – 2. Ghostapo – 0.

"That was a close one," I said tossing the EVP to the floor behind me. It smashed into hundreds of pieces.

"You're incorrigible, sir," Simon said sarcastically. "That was also expensive."

"I'm sure it was. As I said earlier. Put it on my tab." When I'm proud of a comeback, I consistently use it. That, I felt, had been one of my best quips of the last year. I couldn't let it lie dead using it but once. I repeated it again under my breath to make it three times. Because, as they say, third time's a charm.

"Let's go," I said.

"No," Simon said.

"What?" I said walking back towards Simon in a rage at his disobedience.

"I'm not going anywhere with you," Simon said standing stalk still, turning his back to me.

"Fine," I said.

"Fine," he said.

"Fine," I said again, to drive my point home.

This went on, the repetition of the same word, "Fine," for a while. We continued this back and forth like this for maybe fifteen minutes. We often get into these rhetorical battles in which I don't listen to him, and he doesn't listen to me, but we say the same word back and forth at one another, trying to break the other one into submission with how annoyingly we can mimic the other's intonation, and we often devolve into a voice that sounds less human and more like a rodent mid-coitus. Onomatopoeically, it would sound like FAWAIYWOOUUU.

Whenever we reach this level of immaturity, we look at one another with a degree of exhaustion mirrored only by coma patients. Too bored to continue, we just stare at one another. Then, we dig deeper into one another with things we know will hurt.

"Do you remember that time I microwaved that frozen burrito for you and you complained about it still being cold in the middle but not cold enough to put back in the microwave, so you continued eating it," Simon said, "I intentionally cooked it for thirty seconds under the suggested microwaving time so you'd be unable to enjoy the burrito fully but be forced to eat it due to your extreme lethargy."

"Oh yeah?" I responded. "Remember how you had that pet duck that you'd feed at the pond, the one that followed you around everywhere, and made you feel loved and reminded you of home? One day, after you'd gotten home after feeding it, I called animal control and told them it attacked me and my three-year-old, Suzy. Mind you, I don't have a three-year-old named Suzy. I don't have a three-year-old at all. I watched as they shot it. Point blank. BLAMMO!"

"Mr. Waddles…? Why would you do that?" He teared up. "Sir?"

"That's not all. After the deed was done, I went to animal control asked for the duck's corpse to take home and test for any disease it might have imparted to me during the biting debacle. I lied. They gave it to me, but I didn't have it tested. I let it rot in the back alley behind the apartment, and when your grandmother flew all the way in from England to see you and try to get you to come home, I liquefied the rotting flesh of the duck's corpse in a blender, sweetened it with sugar and pineapple juice, and I fed it to you and your grandmother as a smoothie."

"She was one of the oldest women in England, sir," he gulped.

"You got sick for ten days, thought it was the flu, and she never came back to America because she thought the place was infected," I said, running out of breath.

"She was sick for a year after that trip. Why, sir? Why on Earth would you do that?"

"Because," I said.

"What the hell is wrong with you, sir?"

And, then from the cavernous depths, we heard a scream, something human, something that sounded like Marc, and it said, "Will you shut the hell up and help me!"

I looked at Simon. Confused. Was he throwing his voice again? I was then sure that he was an adept ventriloquist with talents that could only be the fruit of a deal made with a devilish being of some sort. Then, it hit me. My companion. My sidekick. My Watson. My Simon. He was the physical version of a Russian Troll Farm. He was working for the bad guys. If he could speak like himself and then right afterwards throw his voice to sound like Marc, he must be a double agent, working for the underworld, a disguised demon, a masked malefactor, a backstabbing banshee, a poser poltergeist, a spying specter, a double-agent devil, a —

"That wasn't me, you numskull. That was Marc," Simon said.

I looked at him to confirm that I had been speaking aloud. Simon didn't move, but I knew from his quivering lip that I was caught. Maybe,

I had judged too soon, but first impressions linger, him being a ventriloquist would not soon leave my mind.

"We've known each other for years, sir," Simon said. "I am not a ventriloquist."

"Yes, and I still feel as though I'm getting to know you," I said to Simon, or what I hoped was Simon and not some possessed presence. "Are you sure you weren't throwing your voice in an elaborate ruse to get me to walk that way so I might fall into some dug ditch to my doom? Is this your revenge for nana and your duck friend?"

"It's me. I'm Marc. Over here," the voice shouted again. I had been staring at Simon the entire time, and his lips had not moved, not even slightly. There were still. Neither did his mustache nor his Adam's apple. But, still one can never be too sure.

"It's not me, sir," Simon said.

"Are you sure?"

I put my hand over Simon's mouth and listened.

"Really? Are you really asking that? No more Long Island Iced Teas for you if you don't get your ass over here," the voice said.

I couldn't risk that. I would never risk losing Marc's Long Island Iced Teas, even if it was a bamboozle. I bookmarked the conversation for later as I walked on.

"Mr. Waddles…" Simon said again, faintly, as if in disbelief.

Chapter 20

Down the hallway we ran, only to stop short at a dead end. "What in God's name?" I proclaimed.

"I don't think this is the work of God, sir," Simon said. Always astute and annoying.

"Where the hell is Marc, or have you been pretending to be him all along," I turned on Simon, "so you can lead me to the end of a corridor, harvest my organs, and serve them as a dinner feast to your ghoulish friends?!"

"You've watched too much *Hannibal*, sir," Simon said.

"You're probably right," I said letting my defenses fall, but not fully forgetting about what had just transpired. I'm fairly certain my organs would be delectable, and it would suit anybody to feast on them. So, I could suspect everybody of trying to dig in on these tasty sweetmeats.

"I'm not trying to eat your organs, sir," Simon said.

"Huh?" I asked knowing full well I had probably just said how tasty my organs were aloud. Fortunately, he didn't have time to dwell on how embarrassing that thought was. We heard something, and it interrupted our repartee.

"Down here!" a voice rang from somewhere deep, somewhere echoic, somewhere under us. His voice splashed over itself many times, and I could sense that it was coming from somewhere beneath me because the sound travelled upwards. It drew my attention from beneath my toes. That's how I knew to look where I looked after hearing the sound. Directional hearing is a wonderment.

When I looked down, I deduced that there must be a hatch embedded within the floorboards, right below where I was standing, barely noticeable, but there! The only indication at all was the word in capital letters written across it — "HATCH!" — and the little handle in its center. Simon had already been kneeling beside me trying to lift it, but I had been standing on it the whole time.

"A hatch!" I shouted, my aha moment. I jumped back, proud of my little victory, which was quickly ruined when Simon said, "I already saw it. Soon after we got here, sir."

What a know-it-all.

"You know what, sir? I refuse to take this abuse. You call me names constantly since we made it down here, and, and, and..." Simon choked up as he finished his sentiment, "you killed Mr. Waddles and fed him to my grandmother. How could you?"

"You want to know the truth?!"

"Yes, sir."

"Fine."

"Well," Simon said.

I exhaled. "Because your grandmother kept mocking our living situation and your post. She begged for you to come back at least sixteen times. And, the thought of you leaving was too much to bear. I knew where the duck lived, and I knew your grandmother had a soft spot for smoothies. I couldn't lose you to England," I said.

Simon paused. His upper lip quivered.

"That's actually quite bloody nice of you, sir," he said, tearing up again. "But, why didn't you just kill the duck yourself and feed it to us? That would have been much quicker, sir."

"I'm not a quack, Simon. Now stop tittering about. Let's get this Nazi-ghost and demand reparations!"

"It's an honor to work with you, sir," Simon said. Proud.

"Don't get sappy on me now," I said. "It's about to get a lot fuhrer-ier."

"You don't know what that means, do you, sir," Simon said knowing the answer already.

Without answering, I took the handle of the hatch from Simon and pulled it open myself. A green mist lifted from the opening. It smelled of lacquer thinner, sharp to the nostrils. A spiral staircase led down into the basement's basement.

Simon looked at me like a scared animal. Well, his face never has been very expressive, but I imagined him as a scared puppy, his tail between his legs, his widdle ears hanging over his widdle nose, so scared, but so cute. I just wanted to pinch his widdle cheeky-weekies, and I suddenly spiraled into the fantasy that I owned a dog.

He brushed my hands from his face. "I am not a pet, sir!" he said calmly.

"Right..." I snapped out of it. Dogs are too much responsibility anyway. Simon is just enough responsibility because he doesn't require any care whatsoever. "After you," I said to Simon, smugly.

He exhaled. Not the bravest of the brave, but he descended quickly, like diving into a cold pool. He went in so quickly whereas I would have probably lowered myself slowly as a man might into a really hot hot-tub. I'm sure a woman might as well. Indistinguishable entry patterns into jacuzzis, so I don't know why I clarified the gender before. I must have been using it to refer to myself in a poetic way.

To move on from gender politics, I soon followed not knowing what to expect. The smells were so caustic, so pungent, I had to squeeze my nose as I gripped with my other hand onto the cold, moist railing of the spiral staircase, which clanked like a falling kettle bell each time a foot landed.

As we rounded the weaving staircase, we faced something far more hideous than I could have imagined. Far more hideous than a gutted human, disemboweled and yet still alive, with its organs cooked before us in a magnificent feast. Far more horrifying than pieces of sushi being cut from a living human and served from a human sushi bar. Far more disturbing than a hangman roasting a lynched criminal over a fire, ready to serve his flesh as a BBQ hors-d'oeuvre. I think, maybe, I was just hungry at the time.

This was the most frightening thing I could possibly have imagined. Now, I'm no history buff like Mr. Mills, but I do know what Adolf Hitler looked like. The Charlie Chaplin mustache. The hipster haircut. The constant sneer. But in all the old photographs I'd only ever seen him in one attire, his classic army get-up.

However, when we arrived in the basement, I was petrified. The lighting was chic, moody, but vibrant. Paintings were all over the walls, abstract pieces that seemed to play off the lights. There were photographs, too, images of cute kittens in salad bowls. Puppies playing fetch. Colorful houses in a palette of happy pastels.

I was beside myself with horror when I saw a pale apparition, a figure seemingly floating in space. It was the dastardly dictator himself, the tormenting tyrant, the unmistakable ghost of Adolf Hitler except he was wearing nothing but a red thong, fishnet stockings, and red high heels.

"Velcome. Why don'tcha haff a seat, mein Freund," the ghost of Adolf Hitler said.

The ghost of Adolf Hitler stood in front of his latest piece, I fathomed, simply because it was the only unfinished work, and he was holding a paint brush to it, mid-stroke. It was of a Marc hanging from a crucifix, wearing nothing but a small tunic. It matched exactly how Marc was posed. It wasn't bad. I mean, B+, if we're assigning a grade to it, but definitely tacky. Very tacky. Extremely.

"We didn't come to stay. We came for Marc." I was stalwart. Calm. Strong in my tone, but the smell of acrylic burnt my eyes, maybe even worse than the Zyklon B, and his tetradic color scheme was slightly off-putting, less of a rectangle, simply some irregular polygon, an aesthetically cacophonic color harmony.

Hitler walked towards us, clomping in his high heels, fishnets, and thong. His pubic hair spouted around the pouch that kept him decent, a plume of dark curls from all edges of the triangular piece of fabric that held his junk in place. He had deep eye-liner on and a nose piercing with a chain that went from his nose to his ear. All ghostly, just barely visible as he hovered just above the floor.

We backed away, maybe out of some innate fear of a genocidal maniac whose existence had led to the demise of more than six million people.

"Vass? Scared of little old me?" he said as he approached with an outstretched brush, which he used to dab a smudge of pink paint on the tip of my nose. Coy, like he was acting for an unseen audience.

"We want our friend back," I said, "Now!"

"Oh. But, he's mein Freund now," Hitler said and walked to Marc. He put his hand on Marc's buttocks and licked his lips, winked at Marc. Marc began to cry, a pathetic, weeping man tied to a wooden crucifix, bawling. The whole tableau gave me the real heebie-jeebies.

"Please. Just let me go," Marc whimpered, even more pathetically.

"Simon, hand me my Ghost Mitten™." I hesitated a bit knowing full well what his response would be. But, this was no time for pleasantries or semantics. "Please," I continued.

He did so swiftly, hoping all the while that I wouldn't complete another sentence, which I had no intention of doing. I was ready to fight me some Ghost Nazi and rid this house of its annoying Adolf apparition once and for all!

The Ghost Mitten™ is a trademarked item, one that Simon and I developed in a lab. Okay. *He* developed it, but I watched as he engineered the thing. The glove uses quantum mechanics to detect electromagnetic fields and transition the magnetic plasma of ghost energy into a solid state, thus allowing the wearer to touch a ghost as if it were a physical being.

"Look here," I said to the ghost of Adolf Hitler as I shoved my hand into the Ghost Mitten™. "This offense will not stand. You have acted without manners towards the owners of this house by residing here without paying rent. You have acted inappropriately towards my friend here. Bringing him here against his will. Forcing him to endure your conversation, feast his reluctant eyes upon your awful artwork, and look at your peculiarly shaped body."

At this, Hitler's ears perked up. His eyes turned a bloody red, and the hair on his chest and back stood on end.

"Not to mention you killed a ton of people. I mean that was pretty bad, too," I said.

"And, vass are you going to do about eet?" Hitler bellowed, a laugh the shook the ground on which we stood. A laugh that almost made me want to laugh, but this was no laughing matter.

"This," I said. And I pulled my mittened fist back, and I unleashed a punch so furious I could feel it uncoil through my whole body. Like a grenade from a grenade launcher, my fist swung so fast, it almost broke the sound barrier, and his dumb ghost-Hitler face didn't expect a thing.

WHAM! I clocked the ghost of Adolf Hitler right across the kisser. I clocked him so hard it threw him backwards, knocking bloody ectoplasmic teeth from his ghost mouth as he went horizontal. He flew high into the air and hung there. Like a boxer being KO'd in the ring. The only problem was that I couldn't slow my fist down.

My follow through continued with similar velocity, and I accidentally punched Marc right in the nuts. He keeled over in pain, his face shaking with complete discomfort as Hitler's body still floated in the air, his high heels flying off his dumb ghost-Hitler feet.

Simon burst into laughter as my follow-through came back and knocked me right in the kisser, too.

All three of us were groaning in pain as Simon, still standing, pulled out his phone and snapped a picture. "For prosperity, sir," Simon said.

"Dju bettah 'ave jused portrait mode?" the ghost of Adolf Hitler asked insolently, almost looking annoyed that he hadn't.

"I still use a flip phone, scumbag," Simon said.

"Wait. How do you know about the eyePhone X?" Marc asked.

The ghost of Adolf Hitler blushed. He looked suspicious, and it hit me. There had been something strange about this situation since the start!

"I figured something was fishy about this Fuhrer!" I shouted. I stood and walked over to the ghost of Adolf Hitler. "This isn't Hitler at all. This, my dear friends, is none other than Dr. Stephen Mills!"

I reached down for his face and gripped the top of Hitler's scalp. "It was all a ruse," I tried to say with heavy exertion though I couldn't coax the words out because I was busy trying to pull off Hitler's face. "You see." I pulled and pulled on his face, gripping his ears and hair for leverage. "It was all smoke and..." My gloved hand had a good grip on the Hitler mask, but nothing. It didn't budge. "Mirrors!" I said out of breath to no avail. The ghost of Adolf Hitler still had his face. "Simon, this mask isn't coming off," I panted, exhausted.

"Sir, I think that's because... "

"Maybe, the Ghost Mitten™ is broken and won't let me grab onto real things," I said trying to pull it off, but I couldn't.

"That doesn't make sense. You punched yourself in the face with it, sir," Simon said.

"Good point, so why is this mask not coming off, like in those Scooby Doo cartoons?" I asked. Maybe a bit too on the nose, because Adolf Hitler sucked at his cheek, annoyed.

"Nichts, nichts," Hitler said. "I am the ghost of Adolf Hitlah. When I killed myself, I had my best Nazi scientists put my spirit in my beloved dog, Blondi's dog-tag, and your Freund Steve locked me away down here, vhere I get to haff no fahn."

"Hey, Hitler. Shut up," I said, and I punched him in his stupid Ghost Nazi face again. It felt good.

"Vat vas zat for?"

"Fun, and you deserve it for stealing my friend," I said. WHAM! I punched him again, "and the whole Holocaust and all." WHAM! I socked him one more time for good measure.

"GAAAAHHH!" the Ghost of Hitler shouted in immense pain. Then, shrugged in agreement. "I suppose chu're right."

I gripped the ghost of Adolf Hitler by the throat, and I said, "Now, I'm going to teach you manners, you filthy Ghost Nazi, before you continue with this nonsense. You are a disgrace to humanity, you sick twisted weirdo. Now. You're going to listen, and you're going to listen good. Ya hear me?!" I shouted. I don't know if I've ever been so mad. I was fuming. Nothing I hate more than ghosts except Nazis. And, nothing I hate more than Nazis except Ghost Nazis... except Ghost Nazis with Jetpacks. They're even worse. But that's a story for another time.

I raised my fist as if I was going to punch him again. He flinched.

"Vassevah you say!" The ghost of Adolf Hitler said.

"Now. Let's get to work, you Ghost Nazi scum." I threw him to the floor and punched him one more time across the mouth for good measure. BAM!

And we immediately got to work. I lectured the Ghost of Adolf Hitler on etiquette, consent, tolerance, climate change, women's rights, LGBTQ equality, the importance of good education, how to maintain oneself, not murdering millions, the importance of a good mixologist, and proper hygiene. We redecorated his basement dwelling to befit his space, utilizing a book I always carried with me called *Cramped Feng Shui*. We shaved his dumb mustache and his dumb head. I punched him in the face a few more times because it was Hitler, after all.

Punching Ghost Nazis is why I started doing this in the first place. I made sure to explain to him that it was not because of his cross-dressing, but for kidnapping Marc and for the Holocaust, that I beat him so. I had to be very careful to distinguish between the two because I didn't want him thinking it was because of the drag that I was hurting him. I told him that we are very supportive of the transvestite community.

He nodded in understanding as if tolerance was swimming through his veins.

I followed up with a question, and I asked him whether or not we are tolerant of transsexuals and transvestites.

He said, and I quote, "We are!" I congratulated him for getting that answer right, and then I socked him again. Because it's Hitler, as I stated earlier.

He soon fainted. With all the knowledge I imparted, I can imagine he was tired. It took me six days, 130 Long Island Iced Teas, a baker's dozen of Doomino's pizzas, and a whole heap of patience to teach him all the manners I knew.

When I had finished, I gave him one last horrible punch in the jaw. THWAP. I punched him so hard I knocked his jaw from his face. And there he stood, a ghost without a bottom jaw. Uglier than ever. Still, he was grateful.

"Sank you, fah everysing, Dahn," the ghost of Adolf Hitler said. "Fah teaching me ze right from ze wrong. I will nevah be a bad boy again."

"Don't thank me," I said and walked out of the basement. "Thank America!"

Simon followed instantly. Marc had nodded off somewhere between lecture 130 and 148. As we left, he awoke at the sound of our feet stomping up the metallic stairs.

"Wait for me," he called. He stepped lightly over the sleeping Hitler as he trekked after us, and then he thought about it a moment. He ran back into the room and grabbed the painting of himself. He held it over his head ran after us, back into reality.

Chapter 21

Walking out through Mr. Mills' study, I could hear the sounds of music playing in my head. It was triumphant, like that song from Rocky, but not the actual song from Rocky. It was just Marc humming "Lili Marlene," a song he got stuck in his head from spending so much time with the ghost of Adolf Hitler.

We walked straight to the kitchen.

"Three Long Island Iced Teas," I said to Marc, "and STAT!"

"Sir... What's the magic word?" Simon said.

"Please," I said and smiled. Maybe, I had learned something over the course of our ghost-hunting adventures. "Get me my damned drink!" Or, maybe, I hadn't.

"Drinks, coming right up!" Marc shouted and got to making them. I salivated at the thought.

"Simon," I said somberly. "I want to tell you something."

"Yes, sir?" Simon said suspiciously.

"I want to say... I'm sorry," I said.

"Sir? Are you feeling ill?" He felt my head with the back of his hand.

"I feel fantastic. Absolutely fantastic. Why?" I said, taken aback by that line of questioning. I haven't been sick from anything other than alcohol poisoning for sixteen years, and I take great pride in that fact. I have the immune system of a third world elder with a first world healthcare system.

"You never apologize. What are you apologizing for, sir?" Simon said, holding his heart like he was pledging allegiance to some nonexistent flag. Or, he was just so moved, it was an autonomic reaction.

"You're my best friend, and I feel as though I hurt your feelings. For that, I want to tell you. I'm sorry your feelings were hurt. That was my apology."

I stuck out my hand for Simon to shake, but he didn't want to shake hands. I could see it in his teary eyes. He refused to shake my hand. Instead, he wanted a hug. Without hesitating, he approached and wrapped me in his arms. I could feel his mustache tickle my forehead as he embraced me fully. "That's not a real apology, sir, but I do accept." Simon looked as though he could cry at any second.

"Ouch, bruh," Marc said. "Best friend?"

"Obviously not better than you," I said to Marc.

"You can't have two best friends. That's not how it works," Simon said abruptly, as if he couldn't contain it. "Sir," he finished continuing a respectful distance between us, and he released me from his grasp. Best means, of the most excellent or to the highest degree in a group of three or more. Only one can be of the highest quality amongst a type."

I looked at the two of them unable to formulate words. Caught between a Marc and a Simon. Which was the better friend.

"I..."

But, before I could finish, Mr. Mills walked into the room. Fortunately for me, I was unsure as to how I might finish the sentiment, Blanche rolled into the room after him. They must have made up over the course of my journey in the basement. My beautiful Pryus peeked her lovely headlights into the room from the hallway.

"What's the good word, boys?" Mr. Mills asked.

"We've completed our mission," I said as Marc handed me my drink, which I finished promptly and beckoned for another. "Another job well done for the Dan Marmor Mystery Box!"

"Dude, I hate that name," Marc said.

"You got rid of the ghost?" he asked.

"No!" I said with resounding confidence.

"What?" Mr. Mills said. "But — "

"We taught it manners, real undeniable manners," I said. "It will never bother you again."

"You didn't kill it?" Pryus said, driving into the room fully.

"No, my sweet Toyota," I said walking to her with outstretched hand to cup her cheek in my palm, her delicate fender. I looked into her eyes, the windshields to her soul, and I could see emotion wipe across her eyes like windshield wipers. She smelled fresh like the pine tree air fresheners that hang from rear view mirrors. I could see, however, that she had her hazards blinking as I approached. She dodged my hand and maneuvered from my delicate touch.

"Now you're way off," she said.

"That's fine. Here's what we did. I punched the damn Ghost Nazi, and I taught it manners so it would never bother another soul!"

"Nazi ghost?" Blanche said, shocked.

"Do you not understand the words that are coming out of my mouth?" I said.

"Rush Hour! My man," Marc shouted, smiling. He held up his hand for me to high-five, but I didn't give him a high five; I did not understand what traffic delays had to do with my comment. Felt like a non-sequitur. Marc can say very tangential comments sometimes.

I kept my eyes on my darling two-door sedan.

"How dare you invite Nazi ghosts into this house?" Blanche turned her wheelchair to Mr. Mills and ran back and forth over Mr. Mills' foot. "You're despicable." She rolled away from him as he bounced up and down, holding his foot in pain.

"What's more valuable than a Nazi ghost?! What with the Alt Right and all. This house is a gold mine."

"I can't believe we're dealing with Nazis again. It's Bizarre-o-ville over here in 'Merica," Marc said.

"You need not worry about the Nazis any longer. They are now just regular ghosts, filled with the decency of regular ghosts, ones that just cause slight annoyances. No longer do they spew the vitriolic hatred of the Third Reich. They have learned the ways of a progressive society as I have taught it." I turned my attention to Priya. "Run away with me, you dear young transport for my heart. I can take you away from this horrible place. I can treat you like the sports car you are inside. I can take care of your every fender bender with a scrub brush. I can take you in for a decent wash at least once a month. I can brush your hood ornament if you'll let me. I'd make you an honest car. I mean, woman. Of course, woman… I've never loved any car, woman, excuse me, the way I love you."

I went towards her, preparing to embrace her in my arms, but she ducked and weaved out from under my arms.

"Gross, dude," Priya said standing at another corner of the room like she was some sort of stealth ninja. "I have a boyfriend."

"Why didn't you say so?!" I shouted and threw a coffee pot to the floor. "Rude!" I then turned my attention to Blanche and said, "'Run away with me, you dear middle-aged cripple. I can roll you away from this horrible place. I can treat you like the chariot you are. The carriage of my love. I can take care of your every elevator trip with the press of a button. I can roll you through shopping malls. I can polish your wheelchair rims if you'll teach me. I'd make you an honest car out of you, woman. Of course. Woman. I've never loved a car, woman, whatever the way I love you."

"I'm not middle-aged," Blanche said, staring at me, completely confused. "And, you basically said exactly the same thing to her as you did to me. Why would that work?"

"I was on a roll," I said waiting for a drum-rim shot from some nearby drummer, but it never came. Jokes aren't really in my wheelhouse.

"No. You're not," Blanche said. She took my drink and threw it in my face. "I'm leaving. Maybe you two can date each other." She was referring to me and Mr. Mills.

Blanche rolled out of the room. "Wait," Mr. Mills shouted after her. "Wait!" Mr. Mills was about to run out of the room like a person at your dinner party who goes to the bathroom just before the check comes.

"One more thing, Mr. Mills," I said.

"What?"

"My invoice." I handed him the paper with my cost on it. He eyed the number with slight agitation and also slight confusion. "This is what you owe me, and I will accept nothing more and nothing less!"

"You sure?" he said.

"I know it's a lot, but this is what my services cost," I said not willing to budge. I was raised a shrewd businessman.

"You know you were down there for six days," he said.

"I'm fully aware. I take cash or check."

"Okay…?" he said. He took his wallet from his back pocket slowly, very slowly, and he pulled a twenty from it. He handed it to me cautiously as if I would change my mind.

"Nice doing business with you," I said pocketing the money satisfied with the transaction.

"That's all?" he asked.

"Understand. It was worth every penny."

"Yeah, okay," he said and ran off. "Blanche!" he called as he ran from the room.

Simon and Marc both looked at me in awe. Maybe of my business prowess, or maybe at my dashing good looks.

"You're kidding. Right?" Marc said. "We just fought the ghost of Adolf Hitler."

"And we did a very good job of it," I said.

"That's not even one-one-thousandth of the cost of my broken equipment, sir," Simon said.

"Tut! Tut!" I said. "Let the men handle the business." I finished one more Long Island Iced Tea in a quick flick of the wrist and threw the glass on the floor. "We're done here," I continued. "Take all the liquor you can find, and meet me at the office after we walk over there together."

"Right on," Marc said filling Simon's satchel with all the bottles from the liquor cabinet. Simon was befuddled by my business practices, still, but I ignored him. If he didn't want to help load, well, he'd still have to carry.

"Another case closed," I said as I walked out into the not-so-fresh Los Angeles air where we waited for our Ubar, which said it was three minutes away, for at least sixteen minutes, but I didn't want to cancel for fear of my passenger rating taking a hit. I take great pride in my passenger rating. It's high enough that if a stranger were to see it they might think I was a likeable guy.

Chapter 22

At my office, we three drank our Long Island Iced Teas in peace. Another job done, I felt invigorated. I was a new man, ready to take on the world. I stood and examined our Los Angeles surroundings through the window.

Looking out over the parking lot, my nostrils filled with the distinct smell of urine. I could see the puddle of it against the window, and it made me gag. I could even see the man peeing against the glass. I recognized the man, and I deduced accurately that the pee smell must be emanating from his urination right outside.

"We should hire this man," I said.

"For what, sir?" Simon said.

"I don't know, but I like his conviction."

That's when I heard them. Footsteps. They were coming in through the door, from behind me. It was the gentle patter of shoes against the wooden floor that helped me deduce the presence of somebody. I knew then that a person was entering the room. Somebody was walking. With their feet.

And, as I turned, I saw that I was indeed correct. It was a person. I sometimes shock myself how astute I can be. She had red hair, red lips, a face covered in red blush, a short red dress, high red heels, red finger nail polish. By my use of the pronoun she to describe her to myself, I could distinguish then that she was a woman. Again, always on point with my observational skills. I wanted to give myself a raise right then and there.

"Hel-lo," she said, with a heavy glottal touch to it, in an accent I couldn't quite place. "I am Russian," she continued. I knew then that her accent was Russian. "I am loo-keeng for Dahn Ma-mo," she said.

"Dan. Dan Marmor. Paranormal Detective at your service," I said. "Just so you know, we deal only in the supernatural, the paranormal, the ghastly. No cheating husbands unless he's dead. No missing kids unless they're dead. No stolen items, unless... well... they're haunted. Et cetera."

She looked into my eyes and pulled a cigarette box from her red purse. It was a box of Marlboro Reds. She pulled one cigarette from it and held it to her red lips and waited for me to light it. I reached for the drawer that held my trusty Zippo. I yanked at it, but it didn't budge. I yanked and yanked until the drawer shot from my desk. I fell on my already sore behind and scavenged through the fallen debris for my lighter. When I finally found it, I white-knuckled the desk, pulled myself to my knees and lit her cigarette for her. She inhaled and let the smoke drift upwards along her nose. I could tell she was trouble.

"I am not trouble," she said, which Simon later explained that I had narrated my actions as I went through them. She continued, "I have haunted bidet. Ghost is peeping Tom. Likes to look at me while I clean."

"Ew," Marc said, handing me the drink he had just mixed for me. I polished it off quickly as I stood.

"Sounds like a bathroom banshee," I said. "We'll take the case. Just beware. I charge... money," I said holding out my hand for a shake. "What's your name anyway?" I could tell by the way she looked at me that she was going to tell me her name.

She puffed on her cigarette, and she said, "My name is Krasnyy, but friends in America call me Red."

"Then, my friend," I said taking her hand in mine and giving her a little kiss on the back of it, "I will call you Krasnyy." I let her hand fall and turned to Simon and Marc. Both gawking at the young lady, beautiful as she was. "Gentlemen. We have another ghost to catch!"

"No!" Marc said. "Not a chance. No how. I just got violated by the ghost of Adolf Hitler. You want me to go again?"

"I haven't even started to repair my equipment, sir," Simon said. "It will take at least two weeks."

"We'll start tomorrow," I said to Krasnyy.

She smiled a big red smile. Under her big red smile, she had red lipstick on her teeth. I knew then that I had just fallen in love. Again. For the first time, I knew it. I had never loved a woman the way I loved this one. She turned and walked out of the room.

We all followed. We gazed with lustful eyes as she walked down the hall and out of the building.

"I'm in love," Marc said.

"Same," Simon said.

"Perverts," I said. "Just because a beautiful Russian comes into our offices doesn't mean that we need to fight over her. She's not an object. She's a person we should appreciate for her sensitivity, her intellect, and her aura."

"You feel it, too," Marc said.

"Like a high school girl with a bad crush!" I said, putting the back of my hand to my forehead and leaning against the wall like a wilting flower.

And then, something knocked beside us. It scared me half to death. So I wound up and punched the encroaching entity with all my might. A huge wallop.

It wasn't a ghost. It was Bobby the young landlord! He appeared in the doorway and clutched his mouth. I could feel that I had broken skin by the way there was blood on my knuckles.

"What the heck was that for?" Bobby said with a lisp. "You do know this doesn't even come close to covering your rent." He held up the twenty-dollar bill in front of my face. I yearned for it, needed it back.

"That's fine. Because there's more where that came from," I said, and took the twenty back from him.

"Wait, but..." Bobby reached out for the money.

"Shhh," I said putting my finger to his lips. "Shhhhh, we have another case on the horizon, and I see a big opportunity, and when I say big, I mean *big*."

I nodded, gazing down the hallway, lost in thought.

"Sir?" Simon said.

"Shhh!" I said, and I put my finger to his lips. "Shhhhh!" As Marc put my drink to my lips, I knew that everything would turn out alright, but for now, Shhhh...

"You sure we have to do this all over again, bro?" Marc asked.

"Absolutely," I said with certainty. "Absolutely..." I held for a long time, a very long time. An uncomfortably long time. And then I said, "NOT!"

THE END

DAN MARMOR

Writer, ghost-hunter, and general nuisance Dan Marmor is the author "Punching Ghost Nazis." But, that's not all. He received a BA from Stanford in Creative Writing, an MFA from NYU in Dramatic Writing, and an MS from St. John's University in Education. He has worked everywhere from chicken farming to banking. He has written for animation on Cartoon Network and hopes to continue to create writing for the world of television and film in the coming years. The next installation of <u>The Dan Marmor Mystery Box</u> will be taking place in the White House. Stay tuned!

BOO!

www.ingramcontent.com/pod-product-compliance
Lightning Source LLC
Chambersburg PA
CBHW030035030726
47500CB00001B/125